The Allure of

DEATH

ISBN: 979-8-9936685-0-5

For Jeff

Trigger Warning

-In the context of the killer: using religious trauma and mental illness as an excuse for violent acts against others

-Visible representations of internalized misogyny and homophobia

-Explicit assault, sexual assault, death and domestic violence

-Allusions and effects of various mental health disorders, abuse and emotional trauma

-Gun violence

-Cult centered child abuse and trafficking referenced, not shown or described

Authors' note

Full disclosure: this is my first time writing in the genre of horror/thriller-y. The experience was nothing short of chaotic as I came up with the idea of a personal writing challenge on my way to Hershey Parks Horror Nights, thinking to myself:

"Wouldn't it be crazy if I wrote a quick little Halloween story about a scarer who was actually a killer, and no one knew it because of the setting?"

And now here we are.

Most of my energy was focused on how to make the killer unique. This led to various creative liberties involving the characters struggles with religion and sexual orientation. I also didn't want to rely too heavily on a legal system, trying to keep it spooky and alluring to fit the Halloween vibe. That's how I wound up with a Gen X witch and her two cats on his tail.

As always, I want my stories to deliver a sense of entertainment and enjoyment. **If at any time while reading it becomes too much:** close the book. Deadass DNF it. Your mental health is always more important than my stories.

With grace, love, and a fair amount of chaos,

Nightshade

1 DARCY

Nothing ever happened in
Bellbrook. That was its charm—and its
most dulling feature wrapped up snugly.
We were a small town, barely grasping
at the edges of the suburbs before our
cornfields gave way to miles of wild
country. And not wild in the fun sense of
hiking trails or rivers to run on. Wild as
in packs of coyotes facing off with
mountain lions, or worse things. In the
shadow of Appalachia, you pretend to
not see a lot to keep your wits about you.

Especially at this time of year. I
felt the veil thinning weeks ago, the
Earth shifting beneath my feet, and had
been waiting anxiously for my favorite
version of death.

Paper thin leaves whispering against one another coaxed me awake this morning, and I knew it was finally time. October eighth, six days earlier than last year, and the trees around my house trembled against the world, mimicking fire. A thrill went through me as I sipped my morning coffee, pleasantly surprised to see more of them taking on a bloodied hue rather than a burnt one like last year. I was being spoiled by my maker.

Gin and Tonic, my familiars, purred around my ankles, eyes also tracking the world outside through the sliding glass doors. They were sisters from the same litter I helped the neighbors barn cat deliver a few years ago. Gin was the first born, and pure black. Tonic was her opposite, a silvery white and the runt. I knew instantly that we were meant to be together. Their twin set of golden eyes had shifted to me, Tonic rising up on her back legs and bracing herself against my shin placatingly. I chuckled.

"I suppose you're right—time for breakfast."

With my girls happily fattening themselves by the hearth, I finally grabbed a shawl from the coatrack and slipped outside. Decay, warm and familiar. The dank smell of rotting earth clashing with the roots of my roses, still defiantly in full bloom.

"Damn deer," I murmured to myself, dragging the pad of my pointer finger across the stub now standing cold and empty where a bloom used to be. It was an ongoing war between the local wildlife and I; whether my plants were supposed to be used as an immunity blanket like I intended, or for their next meal.

It was damp out too. I could smell the lingering rain which blanketed us overnight. Made a chill seep into my bones that made me shiver with anticipation. My slippers were soaking through as I padded down the stone pathway I laid myself, letting the cold in the air take root, but I didn't care.

A lone bird whistled out my arrival at the lakeshore, its companions already having flown south for the season. Mist clung to the water and I had to resist the urge to wade in— though the water may be warmer than the air I didn't want to risk getting sick.

I loved the world like this. Quiet. Thick. Caving in on itself until only its seams were left. Completely out of humanity's control—the cycle of death and rebirth would always turn.

I felt a tickle against my hand and glanced down to find a honeybee trying to cling to me for warmth. She was a straggler. I thought they were all dead by now, with not enough heat and nectar left in the year.

"Come sweetling," I cooed, cupping my palm and she gently rolled into it. "Let's find a more gratifying place to die for all your hard work."

I turned back towards my house, spying Tonic back in the window, her sister nowhere to be seen. Typical. The white cat was always watching me, the dark one always watching what I couldn't see.

The greenhouse door protested slightly, the humidity inside a stark contrast to the cooling world outside. Carefully, I deposited the tiny puff of yellow and black into a pot of pale blue morning glories. Soft and warm for her to lay for her final rest.

I stayed with her for a minute before moving on. Unfortunately, I had work to do away from here, selling my soul in exchange for the scraps of peace I get while tucked away here. And at the very least, despite the bustle of tourist season, I still got to work with nature.

The Bates Family Farm was located on the very edge of the town, rolling through the valley all the way back to the base of the mountain range. My family had worked with the farmers for a few hundred years now, using our unexplainable gifts with nature to bless their fields with uninterrupted successful harvests. All in exchange for asylum.

I spoke with the corn, preached to the wheat, coaxed the vegetable and fruit blossoms to turn. I even spent time in the animal pens, working out their performance anxiety and assisting the vets with healing if any of them hurt themselves. It was a kinship within my blood, one of us answering the other, breathing and feeding and cycling the energy of life between points in time. And I was paid handsomely for it, if only to repay the atrocities which had been committed against my elders.

And now little children dress up pretending to be one of us every year. And their parents take pictures and post about how cute and magical they look on Instabook. How fitting.

After giving the girls a good and thorough scritch behind the ears, I grab my keys and heave myself into my old Chevy. I would never part with her even if she finally gave out on me—this truck and I have seen some shit. I catch my reflection in the rearview mirror, frowning at the extra strands of gray which weren't there a few weeks ago. Time, you are an unforgiving bastard.

After the truck coughs to life, I wind down the backroads, purposely avoiding the interstate they put in a decade ago. It was unnecessary in my opinion. In what world should a road divide a mountain? Not even with a tunnel, just blowing it down to its base so people who don't live around here can have a 'scenic' driving experience.

The Bates Farm was already bustling by the time I arrived. I lowered the tailgate, forcing a hop into my old knees so I could climb up and start dragging my trunks forward. More than once Herald Bates, the current owner and head farmer, told me I could leave my wares at my booth. Claimed that his security system would be suitable protection overnight. I told him I could not: it was tradition to re-bless the items individually. To remove anything that could have attached to them the day before. That and more than once I caught the sixteen-year-old girl behind the register trying to steal a salve or moisturizer as 'a tip'.

Nope. Witchcraft always came with a price honey, and a monetary one was easier to pay than what would spiritually come out of you if I hadn't caught ya. Not that she would understand, believe, or respect it.

Like always I saged my booth, watered the pots of lavender positioned on either end of it, and lit the fat white candle beside my little square register. I was allowed to sell here directly rather than giving the Bates a cut; their thank-you for my willingness to ensure everything on the farm thrived. I didn't have to spend so much time here on this land. I didn't need to pour any of my energy into it at all. But not working with this land would be costly in ways I didn't want to imagine. Besides, I liked that my gifts had purpose, and I loved this time of year here.

With everything dying, everyone got antsy. I'm unsure if anyone besides me noticed the correlation between the Earth falling to slumber, and a human's energy growing to a frantic pace. It was the only time of year people seemed to value life and the planet, since they were forced to reconcile with what it gave us before dying in front of our very eyes. If only people could be so aware of that energy all year and stop poisoning our home. She would not be able to endure us like this forever.

But what do I know? I'm just an odd little hag who lives alone in the woods talking to trees and her cats.

I was nearly set up by the time the seasonal employees began to file in, yawning over their Starbucks and cellphones. We had an annual haunted corn maze, haunted hayride, and haunted barn—our version of a haunted house. It gave a lot of college kids around here an extra way to make some cash. And gave us all one last burst of purpose and joy before settling in for the winter when everyone would inevitably become depressed until spring. Goddess, I love this season.

"Darcy Dee! What up girl?" I felt a smirk curve my lips, spotting William trotting through the sales room towards my booth. He was a good kid; a hell of a lot more polite than the other twenty-somethings who worked here.

"Morning William," I say, already extending the tray with the teabags I know he likes. I have never seen this kid drink coffee, or try to steal off my table, so he's entitled to a free drink every once and a while.

"Those are sick," He says, already eyeing my new set of handmade soaps. Halloween versions—hey I'm allowed to play into the holiday a little.

Bright red *Vampires Kiss*: a black cherry and cherry blossom blend. A cream colored *Zombiefied*: a mix of marshmallow and clove. And, my personal favorite, a sickly yellow shade called *Ghoulish*: honey and iron.

"Those you can't have for free. They're a bitch to make." His grin widened, holding his hands up in mock surrender.

"Wouldn't dare dream of it."

"So, what are you going to be terrorizing people as today?" I ask, retaking my seat behind my booth. William was a farmhand during the summer, but a scarer for the holiday. With the harvest pretty much wrapped up there wasn't much else for him to do, so Herald usually let him have his pick of characters.

"Well, I kicked ass as the werewolf last week, but it's a lot of running." True. The werewolf was the main character on the hayride, having to pop up at random over the quarter mile course to jump scare the riders.

"You liked working the haunted barn last year," I pointed out, but he shrugged.

"Yea. But it's repetitive. Do the same thing two hundred times for everyone going through."

"You could be a wandering actor through the maze." He snorted, but I could tell he was thinking about it. Maze actors weren't paid the best, but the job was the simplest. Walk around, take pictures, help idiots who get lost find their way out after scaring the shit out of them. Hell, I was half tempted to sign up for it, but I didn't want to leave my booth and lose sales.

"What would you have me dress up as Darcy?" He finally asked, quickly adding, "No axes or chainsaws. We both know Bill won't give that up."

"Hmm..." I pondered for a moment, looking him over. Too rugged for a vampire. Too young to chuck a mask on his face, he should be painted. I glanced at my soaps, then back at him.

"What about a ghoul? New concept, make your own rules. And Herald would probably jump for joy not having to think of a concept on his own." Not to mention, a Ghoul on the premises would be a great reference for *Ghoulish* to become a hot seller this year.

He screwed his nose up, "What do Ghouls even look like?"

"Twitter it," I suggested.

"Google it," he corrected with a smirk, clapping his hands together. "Alright. Ghoul it is. I've got what, seven hours to figure it out?"

"Closer to six now that you loitered so long." He laughs and I grin, waving him off. It was still quiet; would be for a few more hours. Once noon hit the chaos would break loose, and I'd give over to it till the moon was high and I was headed home.

2 THE KILLER

Killing deer was easy. They were dumb and predictable, following the same paths over and over. Killing coyotes was a bit more fun. They were scrappy little fucks. I even got a bear once—now *that* was truly thrilling. It caught me by surprise, and I was almost dinner. I had to stab the thing wildly from beneath it, and then almost suffocated under the corpse.

Animals had always been enough to take the edge off, until now.

The walls of my cabin being covered in pelts and taxidermized heads weren't enough anymore. I've always feared that one day it wouldn't be. Always pretended I didn't salivate every time someone bled at work, which was often considering I'm an EMT. And I had gotten sloppy.

Patients realized I was being rougher than necessary, but worse, my coworkers had caught on. Against my will I had been placed on a two-month leave of absence and forced to attend mandated therapy sessions. Again.

And the itch to have blood on my hands was threatening to drive me insane until boom: a billboard advertising a countryside Halloween experience.

I had to visit, had to see if it had potential. I was overtaken by emotion as soon as I laid eyes on the farm. It was like God made it for me, delivering it on a golden platter as soon as I felt like the itch was becoming too much.

I went on the hayride twice, through the haunted barn five times, and squatted the rest of the night in the corn maze until the sun rose. That was my place, I decided. The maze was a perfect new place to hunt.

I wouldn't have been given a physical sign to come to this place while at my lowest if it weren't meant to reward me for being good for so long. And I was good. Better than people expected of me. I was helping people, literally saving lives. Sure, I patched them up roughly. Sure, I got a rush at every cry and tear. Sure, I purposely forgot to wear gloves on more than one occasion just to feel their hot, fresh blood pouring from their bodies against my skin.

But I had been good. I was helping them, even though I wanted to make it worse. And then it was fucking taken away. So really, this wouldn't be my fault. I'd found a healthy, appropriate outlet, and wasn't allowed to use it anymore.

Now: the farm. All I needed was a mask, and I would blend right in with the staff. Almost every single one of them in the maze wore a mask, and those who didn't wore makeup so heavy that sometimes I couldn't even tell if they were a boy or girl. It would make this so much more fun.

I felt like a kid on Christmas Eve, walking up and down the aisles in the Halloween store. There were so many different choices. Plastic masks depicting popular characters from horror movies, an assortment of animal masks, an entire wall of the black and neon masks with the exed out eyes that the girls were going crazy for lately. I didn't want one of them though. Didn't need some delusional bitch climbing all over me and distracting me from what I really wanted: blood.

I felt my frustration building. What to choose? None of them made sense for me. All of them were too bright or cut too perfectly. I was beginning to give up. This was a perfect opportunity, and I was about to squander it because I was a perfectionist and indecisive. But then something caught my eye.

It was on the ground, atop a pile of skeletal hands, which was why I didn't see it before. It must have fallen. Picking it up, I looked back at the wall of masks, not seeing another one that matched it, and my heartbeat began to race. Unique: mine. A steely blue rubber with tall donkey ears, blood coating the teeth and soft black pits of fabric over the eye sockets. It was just as perfect as the farm was, I couldn't believe my luck!

Anyhow, that's how I got here, squatting between the brittle cornstalks in the pitch black, watching the legs of people as they walked past. I was scaring them of course, doing the work, not just here to hunt for free.

But I was taking my time, judging their reactions every time I jumped out, hands in the air, roaring and making them scream. I'd never killed another person before, and I didn't want to rush. I was waiting for a reaction that sent a thrill through me. There were several I considered, but I had to be quick. These people wouldn't stay here forever just because I wanted to window-shop.

I settled on a young strawberry blonde. I always loved that hair color. She was dressed in a frog onesie and squealed as she hopped away from me when I dove out to scare her and her friends. This was so much better than hunting deer!

She and her friends didn't notice me following them through the corn, studying them. Every passing minute made my distaste grow. Did they realize how stupid they were? How unaware? How weak? This was exactly why I couldn't force myself to like a woman.

As my disgust with her multiplied, she was slowly growing distracted and distant from her friends, eyes on the moon. Her useless friends drifted straight out of the maze, leaving her alone.

She'd pulled out her phone, zooming in and angling her camera for the cornstalks to be outlined in shadow against the moon's glow, and I knew this was my chance. I pulled the soaked rag from my pocket, silently creeping out of the corn behind her, and clamped it down over her mouth and nose. She dropped her phone instantly, releasing a muffled cry out from under my hand. It shocked me how light she was, barely needing to exert any effort on my part while pulling her back into the rows of corn with me.

Her little elbow whipped back into my ribcage, but it paled in comparison to the feeling of her heartbeat resonating through her and into me. I couldn't help but shudder as a pleasure I've never experienced before shot through my system, feeling her panicking against me. It was utterly intoxicating.

"Shh, shh, sweetheart. It's all a part of the game," I cooed, already feeling her wilt. I left her phone there—didn't need my fingerprints on it. After stuffing the rag back in my pocket, I picked her up bridal style, carrying her deeper into the maze. My heart was thudding against my ribs so hard I thought it would burst.

Finally, a woman would truly satisfy me.

3 DARCY

The corn was tense, and it shouldn't have been. It was supposed to be dead or dying. But I would recognize that bristle anywhere, my eyes widening as I watched it slowly expand across the whole field through the open barn doors.

"I'm so sorry but I'm closing early," I said, the words tumbling over themselves as I pushed past the women with a bundle of my soaps and incense sticks in their arms. Herald was out from behind the main register in a flash, agitation making his voice pitch deeper than usual.

"Darcy what—"

"Call the police," I cut him off, shouting over my shoulder. "I don't know why yet, but just do it, now!"

My legs were already hurting but I kept running, causing a few people to startle. *Talk to me, talk to me, talk to me.* I darted straight into the corn, not bothering with the cut path of the maze, skimming my palm across the wilted stalks as I ran. Closer, closer—

I went sprawling, my knee cracking a rock of course and keeping me down longer than I would have liked. I tripped over something big, and the corn was eerily still and silent around me now. And my palms... why were they wet, and warm?

Slowly, I lifted one to my face, breathing in. Dread filled the pit of my stomach: I'd know that metallic scent anywhere.

I forced myself to roll over, eyes scanning the darkened ground behind me till I saw her. I knew it was a her instantly because the front of her costume was torn open, blood staining her bare breasts. With pins and needles in my hands and feet I somehow pushed myself to stand, staring down at her in a cold sense of horrified I haven't felt for decades.

She was dead. Someone killed her.

Here?

The shrill blare of police sirens made me jump, sound rushing back into my ears and feeling back into my body as I stumbled away from her.

"Darcy!?" William came crashing through the corn behind me, skidding to a stop just short of tripping over the body like I had.

"Don't look at her," I urged, automatically going to grab him by the shoulders to turn him away but stopped short, remembering my hands were coated in her blood. She'd just been killed. The blood was still pooled on the dirt, not even sinking in yet.

"What the fuck?" He choked out, a hand coming up to cover his mouth, horrified. I finally noticed the paint on him, the same shade of yellow as my soap, and his hair was sprayed white.

"This your ghoul concept?" I asked, trying to get his focus off the body. "It's good." He glanced down at himself, at the shredded grey and white clothes splashed with red paint.

"Y-yea." He was a grown man, but he was still young. A dead body would shock anybody. But then he asked a question that caught me off guard. "That's her blood on you, right?"

"Yea. I fell, running out here." Speaking of, my knee was killing me.

"Running out here?"

"Yea. The corn froze."

The look he gave me was pure confusion and I mentally kicked myself. I'd forgotten that most of the workers here didn't know about my special talents. Before he could ask a question to dig me deeper, the beam of a flashlight cut through the corn.

"Darcy!?"

"Herald! Over here!"

Herald hobbled through the corn, stopping short of William and I, staring in horror at the body between us.

"Darcy what in the Sam hell," he whispered. Before I could defend myself two cops burst through the corn behind him.

"Hands up!"

"Oh for hells sake," I grumble, holding up my bloody hands and felt no surprise in the least when their guns were leveled at me.

"You have the right to remain silent," the one on the left speaks, one hand dropping to the cuffs on his belt.

"Now wait a minute," Herald steps forwards, hands up. I glared at the back of his head as he spoke, voice low and calm but with a possessive tint that

I abhorred. "She was in the barn with me all night. Got security footage to confirm it."

"What about him?" The other cop asks, motioning with his chin towards William. The poor kid stiffens, voice awash with shock and defensiveness that wouldn't help him.

"I was working my shift. I'm a scarer out here. There's twenty or so of us out here."

"Well somebody's getting booked. There's a dead body for Christ's sake," the first officer says. The second one was already headed towards him with his cuffs out.

As they read him his rights, I can only stare in shock. William wouldn't. I knew in my bones he wouldn't. But saying as much to these officers wouldn't do him a lick of good.

"Hang tight William," Herald says, following after him and the cop dragging him out. He sends one last heated look my way, one that promised a fight if I continued to push beyond my boundaries.

"Are you hurt ma'am?" The remaining cop asks. "Looks like you took a nasty spill." I glance down at my legs, noticing my jeans are stained with blood over my left knee. Well that explains the throbbing.

"You're pinning the wrong kid, you know that right?" He huffs, like I'm an idiot.

"If you're right, he'll be released in a few hours. Morning at the latest. Now you come with me, there should be an ambulance here by now for you to receive some first aid."

"I don't consent to medical treatment," I grumbled. I forced my legs to start moving, wincing against the glare of the floodlights getting setup on the outside of the maze. We weren't that deep in, like she was almost out.

Stop Darcy. Not your job.

I march out of the corn, ignoring both the limp in my leg and the stares from those surrounding me. I knew what I looked like, covered in blood. A wild woman, under the waxing moon. Something feared for no reason.

Ignoring the EMT was fairly easy, they didn't even bother to chase me as I returned to my booth. For the first time in my life, I didn't break it down. Just grabbed my keys, and went home.

The drive was slow, half of me wanting to pull a U-turn and drive down to the station to bail poor William out. But... damn it Darcy... he's just a kid. He wasn't looking at you accusatory over the body, and he certainly didn't look like he was trying to cover up something. He was just scared.

I don't know why it bugged me so much. I could be his mother for crying out loud, but that's not the point. The point is he was just some kid from the city, going to the university about a half hour drive from the farm. It was just a job, that he worked steadily unlike the others. We'd all gotten attached to him, though we didn't think we would be losing him to anything other than his impending graduation. Instead, he was cuffed and walked out. No young man recovered from that easily. And, well, I felt guilty that I didn't say anything.

I sat in my truck overthinking every detail long enough for both Gin and Tonic to be yowling at the window. I sure picked a hell of a day to not come home for lunch. They were cautious when I walked in. Gin slightly bristled against the scent of blood on me. And poor Tonic was mewling, head-butting my calves as she weaved between my legs.

"Easy girls..." I chide, stripping my bloodied clothes off me. I don't look at the sweater as I toss it in the trash. Had that poor girls blood on it... and I'm already thinking better. I walk outside clad in just my jeans and sports bra to the fire pit at the edge of the deck, tossing the sweater on top.

"....*Ardeat*," I breathe out, the wind kicking up over my shoulders, and a spark comes to life. Then a flame. The sweater alights, burning brightly before simmering down to ash, faster than it naturally should have been able to. Though my property is outside town, I glance around anyway, making sure nobody was out on a walk to see.

We clearly had a killer in town. Didn't need more folks than necessary to know they had a witch here too.

4 DARCY

Gin and Tonic rarely come out with me. I don't care what people say about cats: they should be indoor animals. They think they are lions and tigers, but they are ten-pound balls of fluff with zero self-awareness most of the time. And I wasn't going to let my girls fall prey to the actual wild animals around here or get hit by a car.

But this? This is what they were born for. This was why the threads of fate brought the three of us together, and they would never forgive me if I tried to navigate this solo.

Gin was purring at my feet, Tonic laid but alert in my lap. Her eyes were locked on the same set of double doors

I've been staring at since we arrived. Her ears perked forwards, and she and Gin both darted from me a few seconds before I heard the buzz of the doors unlocking. A haggard looking William stepped through them, still clad in his Ghoul attire. He pulled up short with my girls mewling at his feet, his tired gaze finding mine in both surprise and question.

"Wasn't gonna leave you in there." I pushed to my feet, careful with my knee. The whole cap was black and blue from my fall, the cut disinfected but still a bitch. I didn't feel the pain though as a smile flit across his face, some life returning to his eyes.

"Darcy Dee, my knight in shining armor."

Tonic had already manipulated him enough to be picked up, butting her face into his chin for attention while her sister padded back to her usual place at my side. My little shadow.

"Come on back with me," I told him, fishing my keys out of my pocket. "They released you on probation, gotta stay with a host for now until you're fully cleared outta this mess."

"You don't think I did it?" He asked, tone a little guarded. I held his gaze for a minute. His face paint was smeared from sleeping in a cell, and his green eyes were shuttered like he was bracing himself. But my girls had run right to him, one still cradled happily in his arms. They would have corrected me if I was wrong.

"I know you didn't do it." I turned on my heel, pushing open the doors to the parking lot. "Plus, you could be asking me the same thing after finding me how you did."

"Well, you were at your table," he conceded, his steps heavy as he followed me out into the damp morning. "I was there when Mr. Bates had said so. Besides, I know you," he added quieter, almost apologetic. "I was just... shocked."

"Which was a more than acceptable reaction, finding me crawling around in the dark covered in blood," I finished for him, and the tension between us instantly eased.

It had rained overnight again, like the world itself was trying to wash away the bloodshed in this small town. Herald had to be a wreck. I couldn't imagine how many cops were probably sniffing through the corn, searching for hints of something that I myself had barely sensed.

"Hey Darcy?"

"Hm?" We were standing on opposite sides of the truck, and he was staring at me across the console, not climbing in yet. The wind was tossing his mussed-up hair, some of my own strands into my eyes too but I kept my gaze on him.

"Why did you volunteer to let me stay with you?" He asked, finally easing into the truck and maneuvering Tonic to sit in his lap, tone still hesitating.

"Well, you're from out of town. So I don't imagine you have family that lives close enough for you to get to work, class, and at a distance for the cops to not be jumpy," I reasoned, turning the ignition. Gin laid under my feet, bapping at the pedals. "Plus, my girls could use some company. You know I'm at the farm a lot. Will be there far more often now to help Herald sort this."

"Why would he need you to help? Isn't the place crawling with cops?"

Shoot.

"Not that kind of help," I hedged, pulling out into the street.

"Then what?" This damn kid wasn't going to let it go.

"You see my booth at the farm. You see my wares. How I set up and break down every day."

"Yea." His eyes were boring into the side of my head, and the intensity of his curiosity was made plainly clear when he asked, "It's witchcraft, right?"

We skidded a few feet from how hard I slammed the brakes, the macadam still slick. Tonic darted to join her sister on the floor, shaking, but I was too shocked myself to be able to comfort her properly. William shifted slightly, his thumb drumming on his thigh.

"There's a lot of girls at my school getting into it. But it's more of an aesthetic thing." My knuckles turn white on the wheel as he explains.

"Lots of candles, lots of crystals, lots of poetry that doesn't make any sense." He huffed a laugh. "But I see you working. I feel like a creep sometimes when I catch myself staring, but I can't help it. You play people, but for exactly what they need. And they always leave better than when they showed up. I don't understand how you do it, but I've always admired it."

His hand leaves his leg, his palm warm as it comes down atop one of my clenched hands, gently prying my grip off the steering wheel. His thumb rubs the back of my knuckles once, a sigh leaving him. "I'm not going to say anything to anybody. I know how Christian this community is."

"Country," I bite out, unable to help myself. I shake myself slightly, whether to shake him off or get myself back to my senses I wasn't sure. "And that's not the point. There was a murder last night, and I'm not letting an innocent kid like you go down for it."

"Ouch," he laughs, "I'm almost twenty-eight ya know?"

"And the dead girl was probably not even eighteen," I grumble, easing us back onto the road. After a brief silence, he asks.

"You sensed it right? That's why you took off the way you did?"

"How did you know I—"

"Told ya I felt like a creep for watching you," he cut me off, his tone a bit tighter than before, and I refused to let myself read into it. "Anyways, that's how I found you so fast. I knew something was wrong and followed you."

"Well don't do that again," I grumbled, pulling into my driveway. "I'm a grown ass woman and have been getting along just fine. Be responsible for yourself, hear me?"

"Yes ma'am," He answered with a grin, and it twisted something up in me I buried dead long ago.

"Girls," I snap, opening the door. Gin and Tonic slink out in synch, trotting up the walkway. As I unlocked the door, feeling William's presence close in behind me, it finally struck me that I might have been stupid in a whole different way.

5 THE KILLER

My farm was swarmed with cops for most of the morning. I didn't anticipate the frog girls body being found so quickly. I hadn't even made it fully out of the corn before hearing the first squeal of sirens coming.

Now, I was sipping a spiced apple cider and making small talk with a few other guys within the ring of food trucks which lined up at the farm each day at noon. They would still be open tonight; the owner had confirmed it himself to the local news this morning. Albeit, with the accommodation of police presence in the maze and hayride. I learned with the rest of the drooling crowd that there were cameras in the haunted barn and gave myself a mental pat on the back for choosing the right location to hunt.

The cops in the maze would just be another obstacle for me to play with. Nothing in life came without challenge, and if anything, I was even more excited than yesterday. Sitting here and bouncing my knees because I couldn't contain it.

"You cold man?" My eyes parted from my beloved corn maze, latching onto the brunette at my right. I've always hated guys like him. Tall, athletic, thought they were damn perfect at everything. And usually were unnervingly correct. The grin on his face told me he knew my mind was already twisted up from just looking at him.

"Anxious. I'm not great with crowds." I've learned over the years that it was the best excuse to use. People never wanted to pry into mental health, and it excused a lot of what I did.

"I get it," he said with a chuckle that made me bristle. Then his stupid leather jacket was around my shoulders, making me tense.

"Get this thing off me," I demanded, shooting to my feet. He still towered over me even standing.

"Jeez, sorry." He quickly took the jacket back, eyes wide with shock and... hurt? Oh please.

I turned on my heel, marching away without another word. Halfway back to the parking lot, I realized that I forgot my cider on the table which just pissed me off even more. Another tall arrogant prick, distracting me with his dimples and hazel eyes, making me lose out on something I liked that I could actually have.

6 DARCY

Once William was settled in the guest bedroom, me and the girls headed out to the Bates Farm. I still needed to cleanse my booth space, and my wares as best as I could.

Gin and Tonic settled in under the tablecloth, napping atop one another as I saged the space. I had a bad feeling, and I always trusted my intuition. And even though anxiety made my skin prickle, I trusted my girls. We were the only ones that could do this.

Not that I should be in the first place. The cops were here. They would handle it.

Just not as fast as I could.

"Talk to me Darcy." Herald had approached my booth, but I was too deep in thought to even notice him. His smirk told me he'd been there a while, realized the same thing.

"I've got Gin and Tonic here," I said, taking a seat, and lighting one of my incense sticks.

"Finally brought your familiars over, did ya?" Herald hummed, clearly pleased and that made me bristle. "You finally coming around?"

"Want me to pack up and walk out right now?" I threatened, eyes hardening on him. "My family has helped yours for centuries. Out of generosity. Not obligation." It was a savory description of the relationship we found ourselves in. For a moment, Herald looked like he was about to argue with me, but surprisingly he let it go.

"Can't blame a man for trying." He sighs, running a hand through his salt and pepper hair. "You know we're the first generation to not—"

"Exceedingly aware," I cut him off, not allowing the subject to come to fruition again.

"I'm sticking my neck out, just as my mother and her mother and all the women in my family have done before, in order to make sure your precious little farm remains lucrative. It would do me no good for my place of employment to go down like this. We'd never recover." He blows out a long sigh, sliding his hands into his pockets.

"Whatever you say Darcy. I'll do my best to keep the cops off your back but do us both a favor and don't get... theatrical." He ambles off, and I flip him off behind his back. Prick.

I check on my girls one more time, before exiting the yawning barn doors and walking back to the maze. It's still early, but people have already begun gathering. Eating. Picking pumpkins. Completely reassured because there is a cop posted at the entrance of the maze, and one wandering around through it apparently.

Two weren't enough. I hated how lazy they were unless shit was happening to a celebrity or a politician.

The corn shivered against my touch, also anxious about the coming night. I felt so bad for it, having to sop up the blood that was spilled on it.

I walked the maze correctly this time, head tilting, fingers brushing the dried stalks. I clung to the edge for two reasons. One, there were already other people, and I didn't want to get trampled by a rogue child. And two, I needed to have a chat with the earth. Under my breath and at the edge was the only area of privacy I would be able to scrounge up.

Direction? The wind shifted, tossing herself north, so at the next turn in the path I banked to follow it.

Speed? The wind died, the air holding its space. So, the killer didn't rush in. He squatted, waited. Hunted. I damn near growled in the back of my throat, the wind tossing around me again just as angry.

Direction? I prodded again, coming up at a dead end. The wind blew straight against my back, so I finally stepped off the path, and straight into the belly of the maze.

After a bit of walking, the wind yanked itself to a halt, so I did as well. It was getting dark now, so I pulled out my old IPhone and turned on the flashlight. The stalks stood blank and empty, nothing caught on them. But the ground was damn near vibrating beneath my boots. When I cast my light down, I saw why.

Boot prints. They scuffed the dirt, like whoever it was had been pounding their feet.

Running.

"Got your escape route motherfucker," I whispered, the corn

trembling around me in relief. I snapped a picture and sent it to Herald.

Hopefully the cops would take the information seriously and not just brush it off. The killer had been running away, like a chicken. That suggested if he came back, he would repeat his exit since it already worked for him once.

I sighed, angling my head back, catching a glimpse of the first star which popped out of the darkening sky. My grandmother had been right. I was delusional if I thought I could avoid this forever.

7 THE KILLER

I was being dumb today, still high off the kill. My carefully curated rules were beginning to bend now that I'd experienced true relief. Since I'd never felt that kind of satisfaction from a woman until last night, I was tempted towards places I'd never allowed myself to even properly imagine before.

I'd gone back for my apple cider. I'd apologized. Smiled. Let him lead me into the maze and touch me. It was easy, too. I had been so hostile because he was attractive, so I wasn't going to kid myself about the effect he had. Or the effect I had on him when I took him by surprise.

He hadn't expected the force of my touch, slamming to his knees in front of me because he probably thought with my smaller build that I was weak. Probably didn't think that anymore with the tears streaming down his face while he choked on my cock.

I wanted to hurt girls because I couldn't like them. No matter how good their bodies were. No matter how great they tasted when I had the rare opportunity to touch one, they were never fully satisfying. I never told anybody because I was a good boy, and I knew feeling that way was bad.

And I wanted to kill this guy the instant he made me feel warm inside. He shouldn't do that, especially not so smugly. But it was that smugness breaking in front of me which also got me off. My breath left me in a sharp hiss, and he groaned, swallowing down my pleasure.

Drool dripped from his mouth when I yanked him off me by his hair. We stared at one another for a second, both of us breathing hard and wide-eyed. Then I sent my foot kicking into his shoulder, stepping on him, pinning him beneath me.

"W-why?"

"Shut up," I growled, my hands shaking as I stuffed myself back into my jeans, zipping them closed.

"Your rougher than I thought you'd be," he complained, trying to sit up under me. I slid my foot higher, pressing it against his throat, making him choke more painfully this time.

"Oh, it's about to get a hell of a lot worse," I promised, anger and confusion and self-loathing flying through me. He tried bucking me off him, but I was already dropping, my knee on his throat now instead. Then I smacked him across the face, and he stopped squirming.

"Good boy," I purred, eerily similar to the same way my mother would praise me. It made me hit him again, and the bastard fucking moaned.

"This actually made you hard?" I asked, now fully straddling him. He was—I could feel the column of his erection pressing against my ass through his jeans.

What the fuck was wrong with him? With *ME*? I'm the one who'd just cum because of him. My emotions continued to rage against one another, threatening to drown me. He would drown with me. I grabbed him by the collar and yanked his head up a few inches, hitting him across the face harder than before.

"Admit it, or I hit you again." I demand, hand raised above my head.

"Y-yes," he wheezed, his cheek turning a pretty shade of purple. I felt myself grinning.

"You hate that you're getting off from a scrawny guy using you and then beating you up?"

"Yes." Humiliation rolled off him in waves, and that satisfied the beast in me enough to drop my hold on him.

"What's your name?" I needed it. Needed to know who to blame. This wasn't my fault, he'd come onto me.

"Trevor," he groaned as I climbed off him, nudging him with the toe of my boot. He stood, still wholly flushed but no longer looking at me with that smug grin. I wasn't prepared for the intense wave of satisfaction that came with the knowledge that just a few touches from me could break him down like this. I couldn't handle it, so I just turned on my heel and started walking out of the corn.

"W-wait that's it?" He chased after me, reaching out to grab my wrist but I yanked away.

A lot of people were here now; I could hear them talking and laughing outside the maze. I had to go get my stuff and start working soon if I wanted tonight to be as fruitful as last night. More so, I had to calm the fuck down and get my head straight. If I stayed here any longer, I just might snap his neck in the daylight.

"I have places to be." He was outwardly gaping at me, blinking as he fought to process what had just happened. Then his look of shock turned to a glare, almost making me laugh.

"Are you even going to tell me your name, or should I just refer to you as Asshole?" I actually did laugh after he said that. So, I hadn't knocked the arrogance out of him completely.

"You know my face." And that was all I was willing to give him. I didn't need him doing any research, raising any red flags. And now I had to make him think I was leaving, or he would probably try to follow me. I could barely breathe, sharing space with him.

I sprinted out of the corn, ignoring his shouted, pissed off curse at my retreating form. It couldn't compete with the war in my head. I launched myself onto the farms shuttle bus—it did laps between the property and town to pick up tourists. That was my escape for now. I'd hop on, ride it for a lap and come straight back. I would only lose about twenty minutes, which would just add to the delicious pressure of pulling this off. And I had to pull this off. I would break after what just happened if I couldn't get any relief.

A half hour later I was digging my mask out of the tool shed I hid it in last night. I didn't take it home with me, didn't want anyone outside of the maze to see me with it. But with the cops around, I would need to find a new place to stash it.

I yanked it on, taking a breath, trying to settle my racing nerves but they wouldn't listen to me. If I ever got high, I doubt it would match the cutting sense of euphoria already clinging to my veins knowing what was coming.

I wanted to scare a cop—that would be hilarious. But I already allowed myself too many distractions today and was running late. I didn't get to start on time so now I would have to slip in unnoticed. With everyone down by the barn I skirted the edge of the property. It was dark, I'm sure there were animals watching me, maybe predators. I'd just have to be faster as always.

Reaching the Northside of the field I finally submerged myself in the rows of corn, letting the sound of screams and laughter guide me back towards the action through the darkness. Faster. Faster... faster damn it! I burst into one of the cut pathways, the shrieks of a group of preteen girls to the left of me making me laugh as I kept going. The next group I jump scared had a few teenage boys, one of which I got face to face with. He was a little blurry through the mask, trying to stay tough, and that made my anger spike again. What was with boys pushing me?

"Run away," I whispered, so low I felt the gravel in my voice.

"Yea fuck this shit!" The group took off, and then it was quiet. I settled in at the edge of the corn, listening, waiting. A group of moms and kids walked by. Too risky. Another group of teenagers but they were running. They were too hyper, would be too much effort.

There. A couple. Arguing by the looks of it. I crawled closer on my hands and knees, peering out at them. She was talking fast, wringing her hands. Then he hit her across the face. Asshole.

After he stalked off, I slowly crept out of the corn. The woman gasped at the sight of me, then curses me, wiping at her eyes. Then she froze when I gently pat her head, smoothing her hair. I don't know why I did it, but I was more angry with him breathing than at her for being weak. She would live tonight, but that boyfriend...

It took me a while to find him, on his phone and blabbing just outside the maze. I glanced to the left. The cop stationed at the entrance was talking to the group of mothers from before, reassuring them that they and their kids were perfectly safe. I could mostly agree with that. Glancing to the right I only saw a group of drunk college kids. I pulled the rag from my back pocket.

He struggled more than the frog girl, punching at me even though I had him in a headlock. His feet scrambled across the ground as I dragged him backwards into the corn. I should have re-doused the rag; this was taking too long. I cracked my elbow down against his skull, pain flaring through my bone but it was worth it. He fell limp.

Huffing slightly, I stuffed the rag back in my pocket. Then searched the ground for a rock. There were plenty out here, turned up from the farmers planting. After grabbing one about the size of a softball, I tossed it back and forth between my hands, staring down at the guy.

He hit his girlfriend. Now I'd hit him a few times. Plus... he was exactly my type. Exactly what Trevor reminded me that I couldn't have.

He was clean cut with rich boy shoes, and a leather jacket just like Trevor's. I felt like every nerve in my body was set to boil, and that my skin would begin disintegrating off if I didn't take care of this.

I raised the rock over my head. *Crunch*. Bone shattering. I heaved the rock again, again, one more time. Blood stained the legs of my jeans, spraying out of what was left of his head to coat the cornstalks too.

"*Hisssssss...*" I glanced over my shoulder, noticing a small black cat. Its back was arched, yowling at me now. Probably because of the scent of blood.

Stupid animal. If I saw it again, maybe I'd add it to my trophies on my wall. For now, I was getting the fuck out of here.

I desperately wanted to keep this guy's blood on me, but it didn't make me feel better like I needed it to. It just made me feel like I was covering up. And with that realization, the only thing that made my heart race tonight as I retreated was pure panic.

8 DARCY

Two days. Two dead bodies. And one very pissed off cat.

Gin was a bristled, yowling mess over the body when I found her. She didn't give me a warning before taking off from under the table, and I'd lost her momentarily in the dark. I'd never felt more terror than when I found her, one of the cops having his taser aimed at her for simply hissing at him.

So that's how I wound up with an assault charge; I clocked him right across the face. Only reason I wasn't booked on the spot was because of Herald, paying my stated bail in cash right there. And now my damn knuckles hurt almost as much as my knee.

Williams charges were dropped overnight. I have that fancy ring camera system that would have sent my phone an alert if he left the house. He was asleep when I got back, finally stumbling in around two in the morning with my hand gauzed up and both cats' dead weight in my arms. His delirium quickly morphed to a protective sense of concern, looking over my hand even though I said it was fine. I was still forced into a hot shower, finding a cup of tea on my nightstand when I finally made it to bed.

Now, I was staring at my ceiling, awake far too late in the day after last night's events. I'd only gotten a glimpse of that body and wanted to retch. It was the complete opposite of the first body. This was a guy, and where the girls' throat was neatly slit this had been far more brutal, his skull literally bashed to pieces with a rock.

It was more personal somehow. Like the killer had gone from curious to utterly pissed off. I rolled over, my fingers drumming against the mattress next to my head. Two deaths. Two days. Completely different in every way. Two killers?

I bolted upright in bed, chucking my blankets fully off and to the floor in frustration. The wind made the dogwood outside my bedroom buck against the window, the scraggly boughs groaning slightly. Seems like the day would be as grey as my mood.

Where were my girls?

That had me out of bed in half a second, tossing my bedroom door open with a bang. William cursed, startled by my sudden entry and spilled orange juice on the counter. Gin was sitting at his feet, purring. Tonic, the rascal, was up on his shoulders, curled around his neck.

"Mornin' Darcy Dee," he said, forcefully upbeat as he wiped up the mess. "Welcome back to the land of the living."

"...I didn't peg you for a dark humor kind of guy." His answering smirk elicited the same spark as his comment yesterday. He slid a cup of coffee to me across the counter, taking a sip of his juice, eyes on me. Dutifully, I ignored both him and my reaction, for both our sakes.

"What are you even doing out here?" I asked, leaning against the counter.

"What do you mean?" He arched a brow. "Didn't you invite me to stay here?" Touché.

"I mean what you're studying. Why you live out here."

"Ah." He pressed his palms flat to the counter. "Well, I was playing semi-pro baseball a few years back. Pitcher. Busted my arm permanently, so done for me. I lived in New York my whole life. Always fast paced and loud. My Doc suggested a change of scenery for the... for the depression."

"Hmm... explains why you're still an undergrad at twenty-seven," I muse, not poking at the mental health comment or the failed career. He's definitely dealt with that enough.

"That's it?" He looks a little taken aback, and it's an effort not to chuckle.

"Should there be more?"

"I mean..." he trailed off, looking unsure.

"...What are you studying kid?" His eyes flashed back to mine, annoyance burning bright. Too bad kiddo. Whatever puppy dog crush you've got on me must evaporate at some point or another.

"Ironically, political science," he muttered, and I arched a brow.

"You wanna be a cop?"

"A defense attorney." His eyes flicked back to mine, then away again. "Want to be able to advocate for people in... unique circumstances."

"Unique like the killer running amuck in our corn maze?" My annoyance was building again. Mind still reeling, trying to piece it together. I sat at the table, my mug cracking against the surface harder than I intended, the lights in the house flickering in instant response.

"...No," William said. He slowly rounded the counter, sitting next to me. The lights flickered overhead again when his knee bumped against mine. His voice was soft as he clarified, "I had a different group of people in mind."

When the hell did this kid become so relentless? He almost distracted me from what he said. Almost.

"If I'm reading your insinuation correctly, you do realize there's no witch-hunt's currently happening?" He actually laughed at the comment.

"Yes. I just mean people who may not be taken seriously by the typical pricks assigned by the courts."

His reasoning stung my pride, a flair of self-consciousness that I wasn't used to feeling. But I couldn't deny he was right. The whole system was fucked.

"I imagine you plan to go to law school after graduation?" I pushed up from the table, needing to get to the farm. I wasn't planning on selling anything today, since my wares weren't properly cleansed in over forty-eight hours. I still wanted to be onsite though, restless. The killer wasn't my problem, but my instincts said he would be back, so I had to be there too.

"That's right." I felt his eyes follow me to my room, until I shut the door between us.

"You'll be getting out of dodge then," I called over my shoulder as I opened my closet. I picked out a thicker sweater than yesterday, a rich wine red, matching my trees outside. "There's no colleges that can help you with that all the way out here."

"Well, I was thinking about taking online classes." I froze with my hands on my zipper, thinking I'd misheard him until he elaborated. "I've got a good amount of money still stocked away from playing ball, but I don't want to blow it all in one place. And Harvard's online program is surprisingly impartial, maybe having room for someone like me."

"Harvard's good," I say a little too quickly as I exit my room, moving through my house to the front door to pull on my coat. I grab a hat for good measure, tucking my curls beneath it. "By the way, since your charges were dropped, you're allowed to go home. Girls," I call, swishing the door open. Tonic finally abandons her post on William's shoulder, on Gins' heels as they trot for the truck.

"Kicking me out and running away? Two new moves for you Darcy Dee." William stays where he is at the table, but I'm too stunned to even quip back. My trunks are in the back of my truck; all loaded up with my wares from the barn.

"Oh yea," he said as if he forgot, but I could hear the grin in his voice. "I went and picked up your stuff. I know you have your routine of bringing it home and doing whatever it is you do to it before resetting. You couldn't do that the past few days with everything going on, so I went and grabbed it while you slept. I hope that's okay."

Screw feeling a spark—the rush of wind that just tossed fallen leaves through my doorway only represented a fraction of the surge of gratefulness and something sweeter at the notion. I can only manage a brief nod before moving, rushing back through the house to gather my cleansing supplies. Maybe there will be some luck tonight after all.

Immediately after the thought, I sighed. Nah, someone else was going to die tonight for sure. But at least I would be on my A game. So much for this not being my problem—maybe the cop I

punched might be willing to hear out my
theory to avoid rebreaking his nose.

9 DARCY

"I'm telling you to post extra men monitoring the northside because I found tracks up there after the maze ends. There's no reason for anyone to be out there, so that must be their entry and exit point."

Talking to the cops had produced a headache sharper than I expected. Did I expect them to listen to me? No. Did I expect them to argue? Yes. Did I expect to be cuffed for conspiracy simply because I was trying to fucking help? Hell no.

"About damn time," I grumbled at the same Asshole cop who wanted to taser my cat as he stuck the keys in my cuffs, taking them off me.

"Protocol, ma'am." I hated being called that. Never sounded respectful, just placating. "We have bodies dropping, and then you come in here saying you're wandering around the field?"

"I work there, son." He gave me an equally annoyed look and I smirked. Two could play at that game.

Before he could respond, another officer walked in. Black vest. Ear piece. A practiced smile on his face.

"Mrs. Bates I presume?" He asked extending a hand. Scar on the back, from a blade.

"It's Ms. Bates," I correct, taking his hand and flipping it to examine the scar closer. He tenses at the move, and my smirk widens. "You're a Fed, right?"

"FBI. Agent Thomas McMillian." He pulls his hand out of my grip, and I slide my hands into my pockets.

"Our little town getting all your attention just for two weird deaths?" I ask, anxiety prickling. Maybe I hadn't been too nosy like I'd been chastising myself mentally for. His grim smile is all the answer I need.

"Mr. Bates is on his way to join us." He gestures for me to take a seat, and I slowly sink down.

"......Serial killer?" I ask, dread winding a pit through my stomach. He releases a heavy sigh, sitting across from me and motioning for Asshole Cop to leave. I resist the urge to smirk in satisfaction. Once we're alone he clears his throat.

"Usually I would encourage a witness to not fall back on the crime and reality shows which would suggest that. However, there's been a concerning number of reports from local hunters on animal death and abuse." Well, that's not what I was expecting.

"What do you mean?"

"Skinned animals. Decapitated carcasses. Mutilated limbs. Clearly not killed for meat. A few hundred calls about it over the past year, so I began poking around. Glad I did, was enough reason for my superiors to station me here with a small team. Which brings me to my next point." He leveled his gaze at me, not asking.

"My team and I require full, unrestricted access to the farm during open and closed hours." I huff at his expectant look.

"Hey don't ask me. I have no legal rights to the property. You'll have to ask Herald."

"I see."

I paused. The local cops were obviously not going to listen to a word I said, but this guy had already decided on his own to read into this deeper. Maybe, just maybe he would—

"You look like you have something to say." He was watching me intently, reading me like a book. He offered an apologetic grin at my deadpan. "I have an understanding you've been involving yourself in this case. Finding the bodies before anyone else even realized what was happening."

Tricky, trying to get me to trap myself just enough to pin me for it.

"So I'm a suspect?"

"I didn't say that." He grinned again, the gesture probably to soothe me but it didn't. I only had one option here. To break the one and only rule I was bound to for my own safety. But for the safety of others...

"My family has mastered a select amount of gifts," I say slowly, carefully, each word precise. "I simply utilize them to the best of my ability."

"The Bates family?" McMillian asked, and I shook my head.

"No. We're related by a series of arranged marriages. My familial line descends from Salem—the bloodline of Jonathan Proctor."

"I see." Agent McMillian was quiet for a moment, processing. I could barely breathe as he sat back. "History is not my strong suit, but if I remember correctly, Proctor was one of the victims of the Witch Trials, yes?"

"Correct." I could feel the blood rushing through my body. Feel the dread and anxiety mingling on my tongue into a chokehold of a cocktail.

"Ms. Bates," he said, leaning forwards again, gaze steady on mine. "Are you claiming that you're practicing Witchcraft, and that those skills are enabling you to sense what is happening in some way?"

"Yes." I knew I whispered it. Knew my voice was shaking more than I had liked, but I couldn't control it. Here comes the looney bin I suppose.

"Show me." My gaze snapped back to his, not believing my ears.

"What?"

"Show me." His expression was halfway between curious and smug. "You have to give me something here in order to back up your claim, or I'm afraid I will have to opt that you remain in police custody for now." I bristled. This prick.

"There is nothing natural in here for me to connect to," I argue, clenching my fists on my lap.

"What do you mean by natural?"

"The planet," I deadpanned, how dumb was this guy? "Natural. Non artificial. Untouched by our hands and our greed." He arched a brow at my last comment, but went ahead and motioned towards the camera. Whoever was on the other side buzzed the door open.

In the parking lot McMillian stood off to the side, a few other cops meandering by the entrance, probably wondering what the hell we were doing. I was staring at a tree, trying to calm my racing heartbeat so I could actually do something controlled.

"Any day now Ms. Bates," McMillian called, his patience wearing.

I took a breath, pressing a palm to the tree. The bark was scraggly, biting into my skin, fighting me.

"I'm sorry my love." I slowly caressed the trunk in the same way one would a face to calm someone. Then whispered, "*Confractus*."

A shot of pain went up my arm at the same time one of the lower branches snapped, crashing into the ground a few feet to my left. I glanced at McMillian, and the bastard dared to look unimpressed.

"*Venti, venti*," I damn near growled, my anger taking over. How obtuse could he be? I just forced a live thing to shatter itself for him, and he looked about as bored as one would be at the dentist. The wind rose with my anger, whipping through the parking lot in a sudden gust, so hard he actually stumbled back a foot.

Now he reacted, a brief look of shock crossing his features as he steadied himself. I smirked, whispered, "*Magis venti*," and this time he did fall on his ass. I think anyone would if a dust devil suddenly whipped up at their feet, spraying gravel in their face.

"Satisfied?" I asked, not even looking at him as I crouched beside the fallen bough, pain echoing through me once again. This is not what my power was supposed to be for.

"Darcy?" I froze, recognizing Heralds voice instantly. And he was pissed. McMillian hopped to his feet, clearing his throat.

"Ah, you must be Mr. Bates. Thank you for coming over, I'm sure you have a lot on your mind—"

"Darcy, what did you just do?" Herald ignored the agent completely, stalking over and yanking me up by my arm.

"Mr. Bates," McMillian shoved between us, keeping a hand on Heralds shoulder as I rolled my wrist out. His tone had sharpened significantly. "There's no need to get so physical. Ms. Bates was simply fulfilling a request."

"You're bound by a contract," Herald hissed at me, ignoring McMillian completely. "Your powers, my farm. That's the agreement between our families."

"Not signed by my hand," I argued, adding a bite to my own voice.

"Enough, both of you," McMillian snapped, the authority in his tone making us both freeze.

"Mr. Bates," he said, regaining control of the situation. "First, for reasons I will explain in detail once we are inside, my team and I require unrestricted access to your farm at this time. Your consent is appreciated but not required."

"I understand," Herald grumbles, finally addressing the agent directly.

"Good." McMillian paused, glancing at me before adding. "I also request that Ms. Bates joins my team, assisting with this case formally and under my supervision."

"You what?" Herald had the audacity to yell at McMillian, and the agent just grinned.

"Let me rephrase: The FBI believes Ms. Bates' skillset is a substantial asset to our investigation. If you refuse to give us access to your farm, we will be forced to shut you down for the remainder of the season for the sake of public safety. And from my perspective, Ms. Bates is fully capable of making her own choices when it comes to her... capabilities."

"You don't understand," Herald continued to argue. "She is bound by a contract. My family works the land, and her family protects it. That's the agreement. That's the only way to keep her from running rampant and—"

"Careful with your next words Herald," I cut him off, pushing into his space. I've always felt this rage, always wanted to bite at the controlling hand, and with what was going on, it seemed I was finding the strength to. I lowered my voice, the syllables dancing together in warning as I said, "Insult me again, and I'll sap your land dry of everything it's worth." His answering grin was malicious.

"You don't have the heart. You're too emotionally invested." I glanced away, biting the inside of my cheek in frustration.

"I'm not going to pretend to know the details," McMillian cuts in, trying to alleviate the tension but he wouldn't be able to. This was almost three hundred years of hate and control clashing against themselves. "But wouldn't Ms. Bates assistance with my team, in the end benefit your property?"

Herald frowned, not liking the loophole McMillian found. I wasn't sure if I did either.

"I don't like displaying my work," I said to him, and he offered another smile that failed to reassure me.

"We have ways we can be discreet."

"Fine," Herald grumbled, glaring at me. "Just remember what I can take from you."

"I'm aware." I wouldn't let my voice break in front of this asshole. Lower, I added, "You have just as much to lose."

"If we're settled, I believe I would like to have a proper look at your farm now. Shall we?" McMillian glanced between us meaningfully, Herald caving first.

"You can ride with me."

As they walked away, my heart began racing, making me lightheaded. I crouched back down next to the fallen bough, the destruction I had caused. Death came in all forms, that most people never would understand, and I was forced to endure for the sake of balance.

10 THE KILLER

I couldn't kill the cat, and that was driving me even more crazy than I already felt. There were more cops here this morning, and a few blacked-out SUVs. Seriously—Feds for just two dead people?

I went over and over both kills in my mind. Where had I gone wrong? When had I been sloppy? Sure, I expected police, but not the actual FBI.

Was God punishing me for touching Trevor? Or was this a sign to stop, to control myself, to bleed out the urge through animal pelts again?

It hadn't been enough though. I'd been suffocating every day, drowning slowly inside my own head. I finally felt like I had some stability and something to look forward to. I know the commandments told me not to kill, but they also told my Father to not do pretty much everything he had ever done in his life. If he could be forgiven and welcomed into Gods Kingdom for breaking all of them, certainly I would be forgiven for breaking just one?

Anyways: the cat. I couldn't kill it because it would also be noticed. It wasn't a stray like I'd thought. I saw it trotting into the sales barn at an old lady's heels earlier this afternoon, a white one with it. I was already attracting more attention than expected for the human bodies, and I didn't want my fun to be cut short because of a stupid animal. Cat ladies were fucking nuts, and I didn't need her becoming watchful of the events here as well.

And Trevor hadn't shown up either, which pissed me off even more. How dare he. How dare he make me break another rule, fall further from salvation, and then just disappear. I should have fucking killed him.

I knew he liked it as much as I did. Knew I didn't imagine his erection beneath me because he shamelessly affirmed it. Did he immediately flee to a priest to repent? That wouldn't save him from me. This town was small enough that I'd be able to find him if he lived nearby. Or maybe he went to the local college twenty minutes out. The hard part would be luring him back here to kill because I couldn't just start killing in the town too.

Tonight I hunkered down lower in the cold. The wind was a brutal kiss, and I wished I'd worn something heavier than just a flannel. I'd gotten here earlier to make up for the time I'd lost last night. Stalking was half the fun of it, and now that I'd gotten some reprieve, I was allowing myself to be more selective with who I pursued.

Everyone was bundled up tonight, making it harder to study them.

I was having to rely solely on body language, which made it harder, but again was just another obstacle.

Speaking of obstacles, there was a fair amount of police presence as well. I counted ten different officers walking through the maze, some dipping through the corn and scaring the other masked actors. It was annoying. More than once, I'd found a person I liked, started following them, and then was forced to lose them because a cop was in their vicinity for too long. So, I moved my hunt deeper into the maze.

I'd gotten lucky the past two nights, yanking my victims back into the corn. Their guards had been down, but most people's tonight would be up. I do love a challenge. And to make sure I succeeded I had re-doused the rag to avoid another struggle like last night.

A group of young men were walking past me now, clearly inebriated and it made me bristle. To have that freedom, and they just dangled it around loosely like this? But then I recognized a voice, making a whip of anger race through me.

Trevor.

He was hanging on the arm of some guy in a wrestling sweatshirt, his mouth on his neck as he talked. My hands balled to fists, throat burning with the urge to scream. I was jealous now too, and it was all his fault.

How. Fucking. Dare. He.

I followed them for a few paces, before diving out of the corn, roaring all my wild and inappropriate emotions into their faces. Their screams and the way they fell over one another quelled some of the storm in me. But not enough. They were already laughing. They'd enjoyed the jump scare, one even giving me a pat on the back before they began waltzing off.

I followed them, as what I hoped was a menacing shadow. They laughed a bit more, before slowly growing annoyed.

"Alright man jeez, you got us now move on," Wrestling Sweatshirt barked out, making the group laugh again. But my eyes were still on Trevor. He was the only one who seemed self-aware, like he could feel the malicious energy rolling off me was directed at him and not a part of an act. Good.

I slid back into the corn, reveling in the way his eyes kept darting behind the group. He knew he was being followed, he was just too drunk and insecure to articulate it.

I had to make a move soon. It was a miracle that a cop hadn't appeared yet, and we were getting closer to the front of the maze. My palms began sweating, knowing I was almost out of time.

Fuck it. He was going to die anyway, and no one would see my face again after this.

"Trevor," I barked out, hopping out of the corn and startling the group again.

"Dude what the hell?" Wrestling Shirt snapped. "You already scared us, now piss off!"

"You can go. I want to talk to Trevor." Trevor himself was squinting at me, like he could almost place who I was just by my voice. I shoved past Wrestling Shirt, pulling my mask up just enough for Trevor to get a look at my face and when he did, he paled substantially.

"Guys go ahead," he said, voice deliciously airy.

"You sure?" This damn guy. I swear I'm gonna—

"Yea. Go." Trevor repeated with more conviction this time. I smirked, pulling the mask back down. His friends muttered something about hitting up another bar without him if he didn't hurry up, then ambled off. I wasted no time, grabbing him by the wrist and yanking him into the corn after me.

"Here with another guy, I see," I commented, absolutely fuming.

"Yea well, I tend to date guys who are decent enough to give me their name, Asshole."

Wrong answer.

I lurched to a stop, twisting and punching him straight in the face. Blood spurt from his nose, and he dropped to his knees.

"Dude what the fuck!?"

"That's my line," I growled, yanking his head by the hair and dragging him back a few feet. "Do you even know what I did for you? What rules I broke? What sins I committed?"

"Crazy bastard," he hissed, beginning to struggle.

"That's right," I laughed, finally pulling the rag from my back pocket and forcing it into his mouth. He gagged, clocking me in the face with a fist but I dove forward, hands gripping around his neck hard enough to bruise. His eyes widened, before dulling, falling limp under me and I released my hold on his neck.

This fucker. He tempted me and I fell for it, just like the stupid bitch Eve did. I could fix this. Correct my error right here right now.

I pulled the hunting knife from my boot, yanking his limp head up by the neck again. I raised the knife over my head, breaths coming ragged, a manic laugh leaving me.

And then the corn around me bent straight to the fucking ground and I froze.

I blinked, looking up, staring at the stalks bent backwards unnaturally. Did a tornado just whip through here and no one noticed? But then I felt eyes on me. Heavy ones. Like they themselves were stealing my breath.

Slowly I turned, glancing over my shoulder to make out a silhouette about two hundred yards from me. They were backlit by the floodlights the cops had installed outside the maze, hazy through the cloth eye sockets of my mask. But I knew they were looking straight at me.

And I kept looking straight back at them as adrenaline flooded me, my arm swinging the knife down through Trevor's skull and killing him right there.

11 DARCY

I'd set my booth up but was distracted running it. My eyes kept going to the corn, zoning out, listening to the breeze and groan of the trees rather than to the customers in front of me.

Tonic had been nonstop figure eight nuzzling around my ankles, like she could feel the tumultuous emotions inside me and was doing her best to soothe them. Gin was in a state similar as mine, perched at the edge of the table like a little gargoyle, eyes on the corn. I wasn't going to let her take off again tonight. It was too dangerous, and her mad dash yesterday had caught me by surprise. She'd protested vehemently against the little vest I forced on her, connecting it to a leash and that to the table, but I would not lose her.

"Darcy Dee?" I startled, turning to find William nearly against my back, hunching slightly and staring out at the corn as I had been. "Why don't you head out there for a bit? That agent wants your help anyways, right?"

"How long have you been standing there?" I asked instead, unable to really move out from under him in the small booth. He grinned sheepishly, shrugging.

"Long enough." He leaned back at least, leaving me enough room to breathe. "Seriously though, go ahead. I can handle this for you."

I glanced down at my wares, my soaps and potions, my handmade candles and hand beaten incense sticks. To the farms visitors, and most of the modern world, they were trinkets. Aesthetics, like William said his classmates had them for. But to me, they were everything. My soul bled into something tangible, to give, to aid, to protect, over and over again.

No one else had ever sold anything at this booth except my bloodline. It made me anxious. Reading my thoughts William lowered his voice, gentle.

"I'll be careful with it." I knew he would be, that wasn't the problem. His hand finding my lower back to urge me out around him being unnecessarily warm was the problem. I opened my mouth to protest, but he shook his head.

"Go. You'll continue to stress otherwise. And so will Gin." I frowned, and his grin widened as he successfully found a weak point in my arguments.

"...Don't take your eyes off Tonic." I said, but the cat in question had already hopped up on the table. Her front paws braced on his chest, mewling to be picked up. Traitor.

I grabbed the end of Gins leash, and she instantly hopped off the table intending to trot towards the corn, but I held her back at a normal pace. I wasn't about to fall and bust my knee again now that the pain finally began fading.

I angled her away from the maze's entrance, wanting to avoid the crowd. Someone was bound to see me muttering to myself—someone already had.

"Anything you care to share?" McMillian asked, joining me. The corn shifted in the breeze, easy in his presence. Fine.

"I was getting antsy. The other bodies were found by now."

"I see." He glanced down at Gin seated at my feet, her tail swishing back and forth slowly. "Might I ask why you have a cat?"

"She's my familiar."

"What does that mean?" I heaved an annoyed sigh, looking at him sidelong.

"You ever work with police dogs?" I asked. He shrugged.

"Occasionally."

"So, you would agree, that if a dog was at the scene of a crime you would continue to bring them in the hopes they catch a scent and can lead to a solved case?"

"In theory yes, that's the practice."

"The same theory applies here." I bent down, scratching behind Gin's ears and a purr rumbled out of her, head-butting my hand once before her attention returned to the corn.

"Gin was damn near on top of the body when I found her last night. Bristled up and spitting so angry one of the cops was going to taser her. I think she saw him."

"The victim?"

"The killer." I ignored the snort McMillian let loose, squaring my shoulders. "She'll let me know if he's back."

"Then shouldn't you let her loose through the corn? We could arrange for a camera to be mounted on her collar."

"Fuck no," I spat, glaring at him now, gripping the end of the leash tighter. "Unlike your canines, she doesn't have a bulletproof vest. This is the help we are offering, and we cannot do it properly if you continue to hover."

McMillian held my gaze for a moment, calculating, before nodding once.

"Very well Ms. Bates—"

"And enough with that," I snapped, unable to take it any longer. "Call me Darcy."

"Darcy," he nodded. "I'll be watching but won't hover. As

requested." He sounded the way a parent trying to reason with a toddler would, but he was leaving so I kept my mouth shut.

I sat next to Gin, running my hands through her soft satin fur, and let my eyes fall closed. The wind shifted slightly before dying, its gentle rushes matching cadence with my exhales.

Danger?

I heard the corn shiver, the roots making the ground tremble beneath my other palm. I opened my eyes, sucking in a breath. It was silent. No chirping insects, no flutter of a bat's wings, and the wind died so suddenly that I could hear the rush of my own blood pounding in my ears.

Gin bristled beneath my touch, a low yowl echoing from deep in her throat. I smoothed my hand over her head, then stood.

"Videam," I commanded, voice rough as I rolled the ancient syllables

over my tongue. The corn before me balked, a single stalk to my right shattering in half, and falling out of the way. Trepidation made my insides begin to curdle.

Gin hissed, her claws digging into the dirt at our feet, pulling to the end of her leash. Her head bobbed with each sniff, ears flattening to her head. My breaths were bated now too, heart heavy.

"Videam!" I demanded harsher, extending a hand out in front of me. *"Exponere impius!"*

Gin jumped back as a crack went through the field, the rows of corn at the end of my extended hand falling away under the gust of wind I sent tearing through the field like a scythe. And at the end of it, the glint of the floodlights reflected off a raised blade.

I stopped breathing entirely, Gin yowling like a wild animal at my feet, her scream calling the attention of the person wielding the weapon.

They seemed frozen just like I was, slowly turning their masked head to stare at me. I felt the instant our eyes locked, making me physically choke. The cold chill of horror rolled through me, the instinct to flee making my nervous system cry out in protest as I remained still.

I couldn't tell what kind of mask they wore. Couldn't tell if it was a man or woman. But I knew their eyes were still locked on me, their abhorrent sense of joy building since they had an audience as they brought the knife down through their victims' skull.

I felt the impact in my own bones, a scream tearing out of me as I covered my mouth with both hands, falling to my knees. Gin was still yanking against the leash, wanting to give chase like the few officers who'd emerged from the cornrows which still stood, but the killer had already taken off. Disappearing to the north.

"Darcy!" Williams arms were around my shoulders, holding me up. Since when did I feel limp?

"North," I gasped, feeling dizzy. "I told them they were coming from the north."

Unsurprisingly, no one had listened to me.

12 DARCY

There was a faint beeping, making my head hurt even worse than before. I groaned, rolling to smack my alarm clock to shut up on my nightstand but I missed.

"Easy Dee." A warm hand caught mine as I swatted for the clock again.

"Turn it off," I protested, turning my face into the pillow.

"Wish I could." I cracked an eye open against the harsh light, making out Williams sympathetic smile. "Hi."

The beeping was coming from a heart monitor next to the bed, and it was faster than it was a minute ago. I slowly took in the room, the plastic blue partition most likely cutting off my vision from whoever was in the bed next to mine.

"Hospital?" I guessed.

"Yep." William's hand tightened in mine, reminding me I was still holding it. "You scared the hell out of me when you passed out."

"Did they catch him?" I asked, pushing the thin hospital sheets off me, and frowning at the seafoam blue gown I'd been changed into. Where the hell were my clothes? And my cats!

The machine next to me began shrieking as my anxiety escalated, my hand yanking from Williams to tear the needle out of my arm. Instantly another machine began blaring, and William grabbed me by the shoulders, forcing me back.

"I took Gin and Tonic home," he said, reading my mind.

"They're safe?" I hated how broken I sounded, but he didn't look at me sympathetically. He was strong, sure, nodded once.

"They're safe."

I flopped back to the bed, digging the heels of my hands into my eye sockets. Get your shit together Darcy, don't you dare fucking cry.

The bed dipped under me as William settled on the edge of it, his hand brushing against my temple. He didn't say anything, just let me sort myself out.

"Did they catch the bastard?" I asked again, voice sharper now as I wrangled with my emotions.

"...No." My hands left my face, coming down to punch the bed next to me.

"Stupid fucking assholes," I muttered, shaking against the urge to cry in frustration. I told them I'd found the footprints. Told them to watch the north end of the field. Did they bother passing that along to the Feds at all?

"Ah, Ms. Bates. I'm glad to see you're awake." Finally, a doctor showed up, moving to turn off the shrieking machines.

"Call me Darcy," I groaned out between grit teeth. He was far too freaking young to be a doctor. I sat up again, my shoulder brushing William's but he didn't move off the bed, just stared at the doctor expectantly and... defensive. Jesus Christ.

"Can I leave now?" I asked, already swinging my feet off the bed again.

"Well, I would have preferred you take the whole bag of fluids," the Doc said, pointedly glancing at my inner elbow which was bleeding a little bit. Oops. "But I see no reason to keep you here. I just have a few questions before I sign your discharge papers."

"Fine," I huffed, wanting to get it over with.

"Do you have a history of fainting, anemia, or blood pressure swings in your family?"

"Anemia yea." I felt William's eyes on me again.

"That may explain your fall." My fall? Did this Doc think I was ancient? I was about to open my mouth and tell the kid off, but William beat me to it.

"She fainted. That's not a fall." I glanced at him, balking slightly at the anger on his face. "Now if you can't tell us why she fainted, or how to prevent it from happening again, we're out of here."

I could only stare at him as a warm thread of gratitude wound through me. Honestly, had anyone ever defended me like that before? The Doc looked just as baffled as I was, his wounded pride making him relent.

"I'd advise adding more electrolytes and potassium to your diet Ms. Bates. I'll go ahead and sign your discharge papers." The plastic curtain swished shut behind him, leaving us alone.

"What a prick," William grumbled, reaching beneath the bed and pulling out a small plastic bag. "Here. I grabbed you some clean clothes when I took the cats home. Washed what you wore last night because it got muddy."

Goddess, he was making this so damn hard. I took the bag from him, only standing from the bed when he ducked out behind the curtain, carefully pulling both ends fully closed behind him. A breath I didn't know I'd been holding rushed from me.

I changed quickly, signed what paperwork I needed, and followed William out to the parking lot. Silently I slid into his truck, a new Toyota Tacoma, keeping my hands in my lap. The whole truck looked like a damn computer, and I didn't want to break anything.

"You're tense."

"You've been getting touchy."

He hummed, drumming his fingers on the steering wheel.

"You're not interested?" He apparently was going to be direct now as well.

"You could be my kid."

"Is that all?"

I huffed a sigh, running a hand through my hair in frustration. How was that not a fair argument? How was this a conversation to begin with? I needed a distraction, needed my mind off of his insinuations.

"Do you have my phone?"

"Oh yea, center console." He reached between us, popping it open. After unlocking it I tapped off a text to agent McMillian. He'd forced me to take his number when we arrived at the farm yesterday, and I figured I should let him know I was out of the hospital. I wanted to talk about last night probably as much as he did.

William rolled his truck to a stop in my gravel driveway, leaving it running. The quiet stretching between us was a little brittle, but I didn't have anything to say he wanted to hear.

"Thanks for the ride kid." I unbuckled my seat belt, but he suddenly lunged across the center console, yanking the door back shut. I froze, eyes wide as I stared at his face. He seemed just as shocked by the move as I was, even blushing slightly.

"I'm sorry," he said, easing back a little but remained facing me. His gaze shifted again, a confidence there now. "I'm sorry, but if you have no excuse other than your age, I'm going to keep flirting with you."

"Flirting... with me?" He let out a small laugh at the look on my face.

"Yes, Dee. I've been flirting with you."

A gust of wind rocked the truck, leaves smacking the windows in the following quiet. This time when he reached across the console his breath warmed my cheek. But all he did was open the door, letting in a burst of cold which snapped me out of my stupor.

"See you at work Dee," he called as I scrambled out of the truck. The wind kicked a flurry of leaves up around my feet, swirling around me in a vortex all the way to my door. I heard the crunch of gravel as he pulled the truck out, but I still opened the door and slammed it shut behind me.

Gin looked up from her napping place under the window, her dark hair drinking in the splash of sunlight. Tonic came bounding out of the kitchen, purring at my feet until I picked her up.

"This is your fault you know?" I grumbled at the cat. She only butted my chin with her head in response. "You like him, not me. 'Kay?"

She mewled in response, before hopping out of my arms and strutting away with her tail held high. Even my cat knew I was full of shit.

13 THE KILLER

Killing Trevor wasn't nearly as satisfying as I needed it to be. Don't get me wrong. The high of killing with an audience was great. And the relief of taking the life out of the one who sullied me? Indescribable. But the kill didn't have the same inflating sense of satisfaction that it usually did.

Depression sank its thorns deep, wringing my damn neck. I don't think I've cried this much in years. And all over a boy. I was no better than a simpering, pathetic woman.

I steered clear of the gawkers the next morning, too exhausted to try and blend with the crowd. The Feds being here drew out everyone, a morbid sense of nervous excitement filling the town. You're welcome.

Instead, I poked my head into the sales barn to look around. With most everyone else outside, I had the space all to myself. Wandering, plucking interesting things off the tables and pocketing them unnoticed.

Pumpkins and half rotten vegetables tumbled out of barrels in the corner. The booth with the chicken themed plate sets was overflowing with neon red stock. I grabbed a dishtowel, loving the bloodred shade.

One booth was completely different than the rest though. It was covered with glass vials, bright soaps, and sticks which already smelled like smoke even though they hadn't been burned yet. I think this was actually the table I'd seen that damn cat sleeping on the other day. Though today, the fat white candle in the center wasn't lit.

On the floor next to it were two giant pots of lavender, I think. Not a flower expert, but it smelled like the detergent my mom used to use. The dark purple stalks were standing high and bright like it was still the middle of summer. Curious, I snapped a few blooms from the plant. They were real, not that felty crap from the art store. I stared at them for a second before stuffing them into my pocket too, thoughts droning faster and louder.

That stupid black cat had caught me first. I know it sounds insane, but that's what it felt like. And that cat was at this table. Didn't an old lady work at this booth?

Cold realization crashed into me, and I jumped back from the booth as if it had electrocuted me. I couldn't tell in the dark or from that distance, but as I thought back to last night, the person at the opposite end of that gap through the corn was small. Smaller than even me probably. Fucking crazy cat lady. She was on to me.

I jogged back out of the barn, not wanting her to show up and see me anywhere near her table. After casting a quick glance around, confirming no one was paying any type of attention to me, I relaxed. My gaze wandered back to the Feds circle of SUV's and trucks.

Trevor's whole group of friends were lingering there, Wrestling Shirt looking like he hadn't slept. Good, because I hadn't either. I avoided them, wandering over to the cider truck and paid for a cup.

I kept remembering his mouth around my cock more than the blow to his skull.

Instantly, I physically shook myself, smacking a hand to the side of my head, trying to knock the thought out. Then unzipped my jacket enough to push my hand in to finger the mask I had awkwardly crumpled into the inner pocket as I began to shake. It was my only lifeline while I drowned in this.

I was glad I was brave enough to bring it home with me last night. The Feds looked like they had been combing the whole property this morning—desperate enough to bring in a couple of dogs too. That made me worry a little bit. They'd scent me in the corn for sure, but that could be said for all the farm's real employees. The only other thing I'd touched besides my mask was the rag I'd used to—

"Fuck," I whispered, clenching my cup of cider in a fist so hard the plastic snapped and cider sprayed everywhere. "Fucking fuck fuck!"

The people around me had no idea I was panicking about the forgotten rag. They offered napkins and gentle words—I even got a new cup of cider, but I couldn't enjoy it.

I disentangled myself from the woman still offering unnecessary help. She was too close. Too smiley. Smelled artificially sweet. I wanted to kill her. But instead, I outright ignored her and stalked away, climbing on the bus back to town again.

I couldn't be here right now. I needed to think. Needed to plan away from the farm for a few hours. Needed to calm the fuck down.

Of course I would be back. I couldn't stay away from it now even if I wanted to. I had gotten in too far, and I knew I was too desperate.

Furthermore, I knew with a clarifying sense of certainty that if I got enough blood, it would make me feel better. I would get Trevor's ghost off me, even if it meant risking everything.

14 DARCY

"I'm curious about how you did that with the corn last night." Agent McMillian was seated on my sofa, Gin outright glaring at him from her place in the window. Tonic wasn't even as friendly, sitting on the opposite end of the couch, back to him. He had no idea how odd that was. He accepted the tea I extended to him with a small smile and added, "Though a more instinctual part of me has decided not to ask."

"I wouldn't even know how to explain it even if I wanted to." It had always been that way. Our world functioned on a cycle of give and take. I gave everything I could, constantly. So on the rare occasions I decided to take...

well. They were theatrical, as Herald decided to put it.

"How about what you saw instead?" I instantly bristled, acid curling in the back of my throat.

"He stabbed him straight through the head while looking at me." I had to sit, the memory making me dizzy. Too many emotions at once, each more painful than the last.

"Any details stand out to you?" He was being gentle, but it still felt like I was being prodded by a hot iron poker.

"He was short. And a fast little shit—which by the way we could have countered if the local cops fucking listened to me." At that McMillian paused, his cup halfway to his mouth.

"What do you mean?"

"I mean right before you waltzed in the day we met, I had just finished telling the cops he was coming and going from the north."

McMillian was pissed, I could tell. The air around him rippled with the force of his bridled anger. Not at me of course, and my anger actually steadies slightly, his reaction affirming the feeling.

"That will be remedied immediately," he finally said, voice clipped. He placed his cup down to shoot off a quick text, undoubtedly ordering the fix and the review of Asshole Cop who wanted to taser my cat. Satisfaction coiled through me, and I let it.

"Anything else? I'll need to head out now. The coroner called when I parked outside, says he thinks the same weapon had been used on the first and last bodies."

"Would make sense," I muttered, unsure why he was telling me this but rolled with it. "He hasn't left anything behind."

"Well..." McMillian finally hesitated and I scoffed.

"Oh don't start telling me it's classified now. I've had blood on me, and literally held eye contact with him. Spill."

"The killer left a rag doused with chloroform stuffed halfway down the victims throat." Interesting. He stood, patting Tonic and she flipped her tail in annoyance. "If you think of anything else text me. Even if it's simple enough as remembering his hair color. I know you were far away and it was dark…"

I zoned out, going cold as realization dawned on me. Then started laughing, holding one hand up apologetically, my other arm wrapping around my waist. Son of a bitch.

"He was wearing a mask."

15 DARCY

I followed McMillian to the farm. To hell with 'resting and recovering'—I'd rest when this bullshit was over.

Both Gin and Tonic were leashed now. The killer had seen me too, and even though it was dark and he might not recognize me, I wasn't risking a single damn thing.

"He was wearing a mask," I said, pushing into the farmhouse without knocking. McMillian was right behind me, two of his men shadows at his back.

"Huh?" Herald turned the TV to mute, pushing slowly to his feet. He looked horrible, and for a half a second I felt bad. But karma is a bitch ain't she?

"The killer wore a mask," I repeat. "I saw him when I..." I didn't voice it but the enraged, if not possessive, flair in his gaze told me he knew exactly what I did. I ignored the wounded feeling twisting in my gut, dropping my gaze.

He braced his hands on the kitchen counter, releasing a deep sigh. His voice was downright defeated when he muttered, "So it's one of us?"

"It is a possibility." McMillian cut in, all business. "Frankly, it always has been. This just funnels it down to fewer options."

"What's that mean?" Herald asked, wary. Not hopeful yet.

"Means whoever it is works for you, or knows the workers in your maze wear masks, and decided to copy cat."

"Copy cat?" I furrowed my brows, stuck on that, but McMillian pressed on.

"At the very least we have something to go off of when we question witnesses this afternoon."

"Other people saw?" I asked, heart thundering. McMillian shrugged.

"They might have indirectly. Maybe we'll be able to narrow down the type of mask. Give us a starting point."

All in agreement, I let my girls tug me out of the farmhouse. We would need to practically smoke out our own house with incense later to get the stench of Heralds off us.

The Feds had set up a small ring of trailers and K9 units off the edge of the property. Honestly, I was pissed we were still open. But at the same time, if we gave the bastard nothing to hunt, he'd slip away.

So, people were bait. They were literally signing consent forms in one of the trailers. A lot of our own local police—I noticed Asshole Cop signed up—and members of the fire squad were in line. I wanted to sign up but McMillian wanted my eyes and ears unburied and not at risk.

There was a ton of kids from the local college signing up too. Apparently the kid who got killed last night was some big wig popular wrestler, half his team huddled by the food trucks, listening intently as the agents spoke. It was both heartwarming to see the community come together, and absolutely shattering to know what it has cost.

"The first victims friends gave their statements earlier this morning," McMillian said, opening the door of another trailer and gesturing us inside after him.

I released Gin and Tonic once the door was firmly closed, but both of them planted themselves in my lap as soon as I sat anyway. Herald perched on a stool next to a small kitchenette.

"They see what kind of mask?" He'd put on his reader glasses, scrolling through something on his phone. The kids made a spreadsheet each year about who was where and what character, but we didn't know how to work the thing that well.

"Unfortunately, no." McMillian was flipping through a folder, his brow creased. "They said she'd hung back to take a picture really quick but never came out. Said she was gone less than five minutes."

"The psycho is fucking hunting them," I growled, bristling. Tonic nuzzled my hand, trying to ease my tension but it was useless. I was losing my grip, letting my thoughts run.

"So night one he's playing. Curious. Those tracks I sent you were of someone running, like he couldn't believe he was getting away with his little game." The trailer shook slightly as the wind picked up, but I didn't calm down.

"Night two was an emotional fucking meltdown like a kid that didn't get what they wanted." I hated being inside, hated not being able to see or feel what the earth was trying to tell me, so I was just vomiting up everything I'd been feeling.

"And last night? Last night was a personal kill. He knew that kid. If it was a thrill kill he would have bolted as soon as I found him." I looked up at McMillian, ignoring the scorch of Heralds gaze hitting my skin. McMillian though was calm, watching me thoughtfully even as the lights in the trailer began to flicker.

"You keep saying he," McMillian finally said, leaning back in his seat. "What makes you think that?"

"Most violent crimes are committed by men. And the way he's devolving isn't the way a woman would lose her mind. He's acting on boiling emotions, and historically, men can't control their emotions worth a damn meanwhile for women it's the basis of our survival in many cases."

The front windshield of the trailer shattered, glass spewing out across the dashboard. I was gasping for breath and didn't even realize it, the air around me static with electricity.

Gin just yawned on my lap, and Tonic began licking my palm, finally calming my heart rate.

Herald was looking at me as if he was seeing me for the first time. A little wondrous. A little afraid. McMillian had already stood, examining the busted window and when he turned around I sank in my seat.

"...Sorry."

"Insurance will cover it." I gaped at him, and that grin of his returned, leaving me speechless.

"Now," He slapped his hands together, rubbing his palms. "I do want you here while I speak to one more student. He's a wrestler at the university outside town. From what I understand, he was intimately connected to the victim. So please be gentle." His eyes narrowed on Herald, not me. The man just shrugged noncommittally, and I picked up a magazine off the seat beside me, whipping it at his head.

"Okay! Jesus!" He snapped, waving me off.

McMillian nodded, opening the door of the trailer and shouting out to one of his men. A few moments later, a massive kid was pushing through the narrow door, shaking the agents hand. He cast a wary glance at the broken windshield as he sat next to me, probably assuming the woman present was the least threatening. If only he knew, the poor thing.

"I understand you were close with the victim," McMillian said gently, taking a seat across from us. "I truly give you my condolences, son."

"Thank you." The boys voice was raw, his eyes puffy from a lack of sleep and excess of tears. Tonic ambled off my lap, and he flinched when she pushed her way onto his, laying down and purring gently. Good girl.

"Can you share with how you knew the victim?" McMillian asked, pushing on.

"Trevor and I are the captains of the wrestling team. Been roommates for four years. Never without one another."

"So, you would know his mannerisms quite well then I'd assume?" The kid nodded, his fingers running stiffly down Tonics back. "Can you tell me everything about the last time you saw him?"

"We were out with the guys, bar hopping a bit. Tipsy by the time we got here."

"Did anything unusual happen before you realized he was missing?"

"He didn't go missing." The three of us tensed instantly, Gins eyes fluttering open too. "I... He walked off with some scarer. The way they talked was like they knew one another. And the guy wasn't happy."

My nervous system lit on fire, screaming and scratching through me but I held still as he kept talking.

"Frankly, I was pissed too. We've been fighting more often recently. I knew he was... uh... having other company," he worded awkwardly, clearly not wanting to be judged or out them. "I just didn't know I'd have to deal with one of the punks face to face. I think he knew I was going to throw hands if the guy kept following us, so he stepped off with him to talk it out I think."

"And when he came back?" McMillian asked and I could have face palmed. The kids voice was quiet, rough.

"He didn't."

McMillian sat forward, his elbows on his knees. "I know it's hard but you need to tell me everything you might remember about this person he went off with. I'm assuming it was another man?"

Of fucking course it was, I already told you that.

"He was a scrawny fucker. Walking around with the kind of God complex that gives you second hand embarrassment."

"Do you remember any facial features? Complexion or hair color?"

"Nah." The kid leaned back, his hand stilling on Tonic. "Dude had on a mask. Some kind of demonic donkey thing."

Bingo.

There was so much tension in my body I was stunned another window didn't burst while McMillian finished up with the kid. We were all silent for a beat once the door shut behind him, Gin hopping off me to stretch and then tackle her sister.

"Mr. Bates," McMillians voice was cold. "I'm going to need the names and addresses of all your employees who may have worn that mask in the past two weeks."

"I can't give that to you." I whipped my head to look at Herald, eyes wide. But the man was frozen, horror seeping out of every pore as he stared at his phone, hands shaking.

"We don't have a character like that in my charts."

16 DARCY

It was full balls to the wall now. Each of our seasonal kids were accounted for, and all the other employees checked in with an agent. Every single one of us was able to either show our costume or confirm our roles as sellers, drivers, or customer service within an hour.

It wasn't one of us. We had a fucking serial killer in our town. I had been trying to talk myself into ignoring it.

"Darcy!" Williams voice cut through my raging thoughts. I felt like a tide was physically rising and breaking in me, barely able to stay afloat in my own head.

"What are you doing here?" I snapped, jumping to my feet and flying around the corner of my booth to meet him. He had to go. The killer had already murdered two men. And they had similar heights and builds as William. If he decides to hunt for a blonde instead of a brunette—

"Darcy, breathe." Williams hands were on my shoulders and I instantly sucked in a breath. The barn doors slammed against the side of the building, rattling the chains that had them tied open. Slowly, I settled, the gusts of wind dying down as I calmed myself, and evened out my heartrate. Williams lips quirked into a half smile when I started to lean away. "That's my girl."

"Go home." I spat it out, almost like one of my cats. William arched a brow.

"Nope." He slid his hands in his pockets, nonchalant despite the chaos ensuing around us. Since everyone on the premises was cleared, the Feds were trying to get us staged and set up early, wanting everything to be running smooth and normal by the time this lunatic arrived.

McMillian was convinced he was inexperienced. I was less sure, seeing firsthand how he didn't hesitate to take a life. And my heart started racing all over again as I realized he might target William simply because I caught him. He was younger than me, definitely had better eyes in the dark, and my face hadn't been covered.

"Ah ah, not again." William's hands cupped my cheeks this time, snapping me back to the present instantly. Everything was quiet, like I'd been submerged under water. His eyes flickered with a sense of understanding, and rather than continuing to push me, he placed a soft kiss to my temple and then let me go.

"Please tell me you weren't an idiot and signed up as a volunteer," I groaned out. Turning back to my table I continued what I was doing before, completely rearranging the setup to pass the time and work out my nerves.

"I did not." William watched me for a minute, then went to the other side of the table, helping me without being asked. Tonic hopped up, finding her new favorite place on his shoulder again. He outwardly laughed at the frown on my face.

"Then why are you here?"

"Because someone's gotta keep an eye on you." My frown deepened and he snorted. "Not like that. I don't know what stick Herald has up his ass when it comes to you, but he's a dick, not a help. And McMillian is doing a job. You need me."

"I don't need anyone." He smirked.

"You need Gin and Tonic." Tonic knocked her head into the back of his, purring loudly.

"That's different. It's a bond we share through fate."

"It's the same and you know it." I opened my mouth to argue but he shut me up with a look, leaning almost close enough to touch. "Same way I know you're going to catch the guy tonight."

Tonic hopped down on the table again, mewing for me to pick her up now so I did. I cradled her like a damn baby, staring out the barn doors.

"What if I don't?" I whispered, fear making me cold.

William just stooped over, plucking Gin from the ground as she asked for a rare dose of affection. He grinned at me over her head when she started purring.

"You will."

I took a breath, feeling the ebb and flow of the earth around me. The smell of decay heavier now as we plunged closer to winter. There was a rumble of distant thunder, low enough to mistake for a plane.

"I will if these fuckers finally cover the north end of the field." William laughed.

17 THE KILLER

It had been raining on and off all afternoon, but it was exactly the kind of cleansing I needed.

With my head clear, I came up with a feasible plan this time. There were too many eyes now, so I would need to be strategic. That's why I had walked the mountain for a few miles, reaching the woods which backed the property way before the sun had set behind the building dark clouds. I never was caught leaving, but I didn't need anyone to see me coming this time either.

Tonight would be my last night. Here at least. It would do me no good to linger where Trevor's ghost was. And I had no doubt that I would be able to find another place like this if I had to, to keep blowing off steam. He made me realize that I needed to release all the pent-up anguish and confusion in me before it ate me alive.

Other people got to heal right? Other people got to release and do what they needed to stop finally feeling pain, so why wasn't I allowed to? God wouldn't have presented me with the perfect opportunity to act otherwise.

A sense of melancholy settled over me as I watched the corn sway against itself, a beckoning melody for me. Everything was perfect; the clouds blocking out the moon so that the only lights trying to catch me would be the glare from the iridescent floodlights the cops continued to use.

I pulled my mask on, inhaling the scent of the wet night through the rubber. Pausing in the embrace of the dark, wanting to cling to this moment forever. It was misting lightly, reflecting off a dull silver in the dark. Hauntingly beautiful.

A perfect night to hunt.

I moved even slower than other nights, my head tilted as I walked to listen. I had gotten good at it; my hearing heightened in the dark. The crowd was smaller than normal, the impending storm and my antics keeping people at bay. At least they had survival instincts. Made me less mad at them for not being what I needed them to be. Speaking of.

I pulled the bruised purple blooms from my coat, pressing them to the mask and inhaling deeply. They reeked, but it was a fabulous little personal note I would leave behind. Adrenaline flooded me already as I pictured her face. She was probably so cocky right now. Probably talked to the cops for hours, grasping at her five seconds of fame with her damn cats.

For that, I wanted two tonight. One boy and one girl. One that I shouldn't want, and one that I couldn't force myself to want no matter what I did. Two kills in one night would be enough to erase what Trevor did to me. It has to be.

I kept my new rag tucked away inside my back pocket. I was a little worried that the impending rain would dilute the dose—I would need it in top shape if it was going to be used twice. But at this point I was getting annoyed that I wouldn't be able to use it at all.

Groups of people were wandering through the maze. Small, and huddled together because of the weather. I would just have to try harder.

I dove out in front of a group of girls, their screams so high pitched it made my ears hurt. One began crying but the other... no way.

"Don't do that," I growled, whipping my knife out. She still managed to blow into the whistle she'd raised before I grabbed her by the throat. Her friends froze as I brought the blade level with her neck.

They knew. The whistle was to catch me. Panic thudded through me, but I still had control of the situation. I could still get what I needed.

"Run," I demanded. I changed the angle of the knife, and knew blood was rolling down her neck when she released a pained whimper. "I'll slit her throat right here, you know it. So go ahead, scream and run."

"Go to hell," one whispered, backing away with her voice shaking. Her other friend had already darted away, and I laughed. Then sank the blade into the girl's neck.

Her body thrashed against mine, choking, squirming, and I groaned in satisfaction. I kept her pressed tightly to me while her body writhed, feeling every shudder and jerk, and how they were slowing. I drank in the look of horror on her friends face, releasing a satisfied laugh when she fell to her knees, screaming as her friend went limp in my arms.

I dropped her in the mud, stepping back. Dug my free hand into my pocket, fisting the wilted petals and sprinkled them over her body. Her friend blew her whistle then, but I didn't care anymore. I felt like a God.

The rush was short lived, a gunshot going off behind me and then I was the one screaming, falling face first back into the corn and grabbing my arm. They fucking shot me! The bullet was wedged against the bone, making every breath I took a fight to stay awake.

I stumbled to my feet, blood dripping off my hand in a rush. Just another obstacle, this was fine. If anything, the pain shooting up and down my left side just fueled me on.

This wasn't my fault. I was a good boy and had been doing just fine. My job as an EMT had me in the position of controlling the pain happening to others. That and hunting small game had been enough to take the edge off without doing any real damage.

But they had to go and suspend me. Had to go punish me for something that I *needed* to be okay. Couldn't they understand that?

18 DARCY

I bolted into the corn before the whistle blew. Death. I could smell it. Could feel it creeping through the maze, like fog rolling down from the mountain.

Gin and Tonic were in the barn with William, terrified of the blooming thunder and I didn't blame them. They knew it wasn't natural, knew my sense of self control was wearing thin because of it. I'd fought this for so long. This chaos. This desire to drain, bend, manipulate.

My mother always tried to justify it, saying it was only in our nature to push to the most extreme of gives and takes. Said the earth knew we could keep up with her—keep up with the demand of death in order to create new life.

That's why the Bates family had us on a leash, to monitor this unpredictable scale of giving and taking. Tying our powers to this land, basing our survival off one another. But now there had been so much death on it, so much blood seeping in. Hurtling us closer and closer to shattering the bond, leaving both ends empty.

Power demanded sacrifice. It demanded freedom. And it left you if you abused the way you could touch it.

A girl sprinted past me, terror thrumming off her in tangible chords through the air. It sank into me like barbed thorns, the cold wind biting its teeth in right after. I was too late.

As I skidded around the bend in the maze I heard the sharp cry of a whistle, quickly followed by a gunshot. A cry of my own tore out of my throat. Anger boiled beneath the fear, pushing me to ignore the screaming in my knees and run faster.

I found a second girl, sobbing as she hunched over her friend's body, cradling her head in her lap. That wasn't what had me pull up, covering my mouth with my hands though. Sprinkled across the ground around her feet and her waist, were broken stems of lavender blooms.

An eerie stillness ghosted through the field as the cold wash of horror threatened to drown me.

He knew it was me who saw him the other night. And wanted to make me suffer for failing to protect this place.

"Get out of the maze," I barked out, voice raw with fear and anger. The girl didn't budge so I grabbed her by the shoulders. "He is still out here! Get out of the god damn maze!"

Two agents in full black tac gear had heard her crying or me yelling, because they burst out of the corn behind her making both of us scream. One was speaking into an earpiece, the other kneeling at the girl's side.

"Who are you talking to?" I snapped at the first and he ignored me. I was so fucking over not being listened to. Trusting my gut, I reached out, yanking the piece from his ear. "McMillian!?"

"Darcy?" The voice came to me through a burst of static, but it was him. The agent in front of me though was yelling, and pulling his taser.

"For Christs sake!" I snapped, holding my hands up. "I'm trying to help!"

"All hands stand down!" McMillian shouted in my ear, "Let Ms. Bates speak!"

Luckily, the other agent was paying attention, damn near tackling his partner half a second before he shot off the taser. It landed in the mud behind me, barely missing me by an inch.

"For Goddess' sake please tell me the north end of the field is blocked?" I asked, a pop of static making me jump. My head was on a swivel, and I kept turning slowly round and round, eyes not leaving the corn for a second.

"Thirty men stationed along the north end of the property," McMillian finally responded, and I breathed a sigh of relief. "If he runs, we're ready."

"Good," I said, bracing myself as I immediately added. "Get everyone out of the maze." A beat of silence.

"What?"

"Get everyone out of the maze," I repeated, hands shaking, body already rejecting the plan I had come up with. "We know he's in here. He'll either run by the time everyone clears out, or if he keeps hiding... I can get him."

Another long pause, this one making me feel like I was going to be cut off for good. I had no authority here. No training. No damn reason for them to listen to me. My heart was about to burst in my chest when I finally heard McMillian clear his throat.

"You all heard Ms. Bates: fall back. Keep the north perimeter secure and engage on sight. Clear the field of civilians. And Darcy," he said, my skin crawling with goosebumps. "You better know what you're doing."

I swallowed down the burn of acid in the back of my throat, remaining frozen for a moment as the agents at my back lifted the body, her sobbing friend following them out.

I was alone again. Quiet. My hand stroked the cornstalk closest to me, and I swear it shivered before leaning away on the wind as it built again.

I glanced back down at the ground; at the now trampled lavender he'd mockingly graced her body with. Thunder rolled above me again as I finally turned, jogging down the paths of the maze. I was alone the whole way, which I needed. No one could prepare me for what I was about to sacrifice.

Everything was ending tonight.

19 THE KILLER

 I darted between the cornstalks, half blind from the weather. Calm, slow. They'd be listening for me barging around in here. My arm was killing me though, and I needed to catch my breath.

 I squat down, trying to quiet my heaves for breath. The raindrops were fatter now, slapping against my mask before rolling down the back of my neck. It was cold, but centering.

 Twice cops sped right past me, not noticing my small frame clad in black and clinging to the shadows. The only color on me was my mask, but the slate blue would be hard to see in weather like this too.

It was getting quieter, the cries and screams of guests being replaced by the rushed shouts of cops. I poked my head out onto one of the paths, checking both ways before darting across. My anxiety was beginning to catch up with the adrenaline. If I didn't get to kill another guy I don't think I would ever be able to move on from the experience with Trevor. I couldn't let that happen.

I crouched back down as I heard heavy footfalls approaching me and held my breath. Then lost it in a rush, momentarily blown away when I saw Wrestling Shirt flying down the path towards me. A surge of joy went through me at the sight of him: what a gift!

I forced my giddiness down, replacing it with cold resolution instead. I had to time this—had only one shot with a guy that big. And I wanted to enjoy this one, my last.

I caught him by surprise, springing out of the corn and latching onto his back. He shouted, hitting the ground. Smart, he was trying to get me under him, use his size against me but my knife was still out. He howled when I cut across his back, his sweatshirt fraying beneath the blade and his blood soaking the grey fabric instantly. I raised it to bring it through his skull, but he rolled, and the blade got buried into his shoulder instead.

Then I was the one howling when he grabbed my shot arm, tossing me back into the corn like I was a rag doll.

"Rot in hell, ya sick bastard!" He yelled, but I could only groan from my spot on the ground.

Stars were blurring my vision from the pain in my arm, and I braced for him to come finish me off. I would if I were in his position. But he didn't stick around—despite stabbing him the giant fuck was already running again. My kill was running away like I'd barely touched him.

"COWARD!" I screamed after him, the world feeling my fury as thunder cracked above me.

Rain was pouring down now, mixing with my blood as it continued to run. What was this? Another cleansing? I took a relieved breath; God understood me, even if the rest of the world didn't.

I yanked the mask off my head, too much water in it to breathe now. I cried out again as I sat up, my arm throbbing worse with every passing moment. Every muscle in my body screamed in protest, my head spinning as I forced myself to my feet.

It was time to leave. I would recover. I could pretend Trevor never happened. Pretend I never felt the absolute euphoria of taking a life. I was strong enough to do that, I just needed to be reinstated at work—early if I was good.

As I hobbled towards the edge of the field, the shouting which had begun to die down, started growing louder again. I crept just close enough to peek out, and my heart dropped to the pit of my stomach.

Agents. Dogs. A wall, all lined up at the back of the field... waiting for me.

Tears began streaming down my face, mixing with the rain. A frustrated wail ripped from me as I turned around, trudging back into the corn to hide. And then laughter, hot and desperate.

Their shouts grew louder, probably hearing me. I sank back to the ground as the beams of their flashlights cut between the stalks, seeking me out. The dogs would find me. Tear me apart. I couldn't stop crying. I deserved better than that. This wasn't my fault!

But then everything went still. The rain stopped. The world fell quiet. I was on my knees, and when I was brave enough to lift my head, the sky went white above me.

And heaven crashed down to claim me.

20 DARCY

I had barely been holding the storm back to begin with, and by the time I broke out of the maze lightning was kissing the boiling clouds above. I caught sight of Herald surrounded by a throng of people. The farms employees were scattered around under the floodlights, taking a headcount of all the volunteers. Even from this far away his eyes on mine were livid, but for the first time in my life, I wasn't afraid of what he would do.

"You have the Northside of the field covered?" I asked for the millionth time.

"Secured." McMillian responded in my ear, the same as the other four times. "What do you need?" I hesitated, weighing how much to tell him. But people were dying, and I could stop it.

"You ordered your men to shoot on sight... right?"

"We got a shot fired at him shortly after the whistle," McMillian said, words measured. I knew that but didn't interrupt. "I doubt we'll get another, unless he runs."

"And if one of them did, and the shot killed him?" I could barely breathe. "They would just be doing their job, right? Not criminalized for the measures they took to stop him?"

"No," McMillian said, voice grave. "They would not be criminalized." I forced myself to swallow down the rising nausea.

"And if I did my version of that?"

I was pacing now, fists clenched in the rain. The ground was withering at my feet, half-dead grass fading to black, the roots crumbling and churning beneath the dirt. But McMillian's voice was steady in his reply.

"Then you would be aiding my team in catching this lunatic." I released a breath I hadn't known I'd been holding, my heart thudding in my chest. "Tell me what you need Ms. Bates," McMillian said, and I lifted my head, forcing conviction back in my tone.

"Get everyone out of the maze."

People had been pouring out long before I had got out. For a moment, I watched them. Every move was pure instinct taking over for once, and I marveled at it. Perhaps humans haven't grown as out of touch with our nature as I believed. They just had to pretend otherwise to survive the modern world.

"What are you planning?" Herald had crept up on me, making me nearly jump out of my skin. Despite the chaos raging around us he had the nerve to be scowling at me, arms crossed.

"...Does controlling my power really matter more to you than people dying?" I asked breathlessly, disgust and disbelief coiling through me.

"You know better than anyone what this land means to me," he said, voice grave. "I hate that this is happening. But the look in your eyes right now..." he trailed off, but his face said it all.

"What?" I growled, another roll of thunder punctuating the word. He flinched. It was subtle, but I saw it. I took a step towards him, and the anger in his gaze shifted to apprehension. My voice was low, measured as I asked, "You afraid of me?"

His jaw clenched. I smirked. Lightning flashed, the wind whipping around us viciously. I took another step, invading his space. Every ounce of repressed anger, guilt, fear, and self-sabotage made the air between us crackle with static.

"I'm done letting you control my bloodline. Or did you think my refusal to marry you and procreate was just for theatrics?" I tossed his words back in his face, and he took half a step back. I closed the distance again, energy rushing through me.

"If you do what I think you're going to do," he said roughly, his voice quaking, "then you'll lose your magic."

"I can live with that." It would be agonizing. A hell no one would understand, but I kept my chin high. "It's you who won't be able to. You will need to learn how to nurture your land yourself, instead of relying on me to drain myself dry for you year after year."

Herald was pale, his jaw having gone slack while I spoke. I turned my back on him, poking the piece of tech in my ear again.

"Is everyone out of the corn?" I asked, the build up in me beginning to burn. The tension in the air was popping now, threads of electricity threading between my fingers. I felt Herald move away from me, his fear making the air taste sweet. Almost sweet enough to make me forget about what I was going to lose.

"Tell me when everyone's out." I could only whisper now, but McMillian heard me. He kept shouting orders, calling in checks, while I compressed down into myself.

Everything stilled.

The rushing heartbeat slamming through my chest was not my own. The earth was pulsing in my very veins, every element, every atom. It was a mess, and while I was frantic, I was secure. This was my land, my power, and my duty.

I walked to the edge of the corn, kneeling before it. My palms gently caressed the dirt at my feet, remorse wafting off me. Thunder rolled with my next shuddered breath, and the whole field shivered as it felt the intention in my touch.

"I'm so sorry, my precious darling," I whispered, letting my tears fall this time. They mixed with the weight of the rain soaking the soil, dragging my reach deeper still. Sadness was energy too, and I needed all of it. "You deserve better than this."

The ground beneath me had stopped trembling, the wind at my back soft, the corn sagging forwards in a farewell I didn't know how to describe but felt deep to the pit of my core. We were tied to one another, in a cycle of give and take that we knew would eventually be spent. The unspoken understanding crossed between us through the veil, and the rain started pelting down. The world crying with me.

"Twenty seconds till we're clear!" McMillian shouted in my ear, and I forced myself to breathe. Twenty seconds. I had that much control left. I could do this.

But it burned, like acid whipping through my veins. My own magic was fighting me, against what I was planning to do. I called down more, forcing myself to welcome the burn as I took what wasn't mine. I bridled the storm to myself, my tears mixing with its essence.

"McMillian?" I sobbed, my entire body going taut. My arms rose above my head as the energy they were tethered to demanded more of me, blood running from my nose in payment for what I was stealing.

"Ten seconds!"

Breathe. Even if you're sobbing. Even if you're breaking.

"Five seconds!"

Everything you've ever repressed, everything you've ever buried—

"Two seconds!"

"I'm so sorry my love," I whisper again. And then release.

The field lights up, the sky blazing a brilliant white. A rain of lightning strikes come crashing down

169

into the center of the maze, keeping time with my hands they slam back down to the earth. The sound is deafening, but I raise my voice above it all.

"Ardeat!" I scream, and unnatural waves of flame break out through the corn, like a storming sea caving in on itself. The brittle cornstalks, so near a natural death, catch alight. The world before me is thrashing, popping and hissing, beating back against itself as the flames spread.

I stay where I am, on my knees before it all. The heat is blistering my skin, but I'm so cold inside I can barely register the flames threatening to swallow me whole. And as it all burned to ash, the grief that barreled through me was enough to make me succumb to the dark.

21 DARCY

...reports of a masked killer running lose through a cornfield in western Virginia. Authorities say the individual responsible for three murders and two stabbings has been killed by a wildfire which broke out on the property. It is unclear if this fire was started by the killer themselves or by a worker at the farm in the...

Everything in me was still burning. The taste of ash still stuck to my tongue had me choking, coughing roughly into the blanket pulled up to my face. Hands were on me, but I didn't care, their heat seeping into my frozen back as I leaned over the edge of the bed and retched.

"Easy Dee." Spoken low and soft, hands holding my hair back as my retches turned back to sobs. William slowly pulled me backwards, bracing himself on the plastic headboard and resting me on his chest. The hospital bed below us groaned in protest, but I was too weak to echo it.

He shifted and I heard the click of a button, probably calling one of the doctors in. Through blurry eyes I found the TV, the reporter looking like bubblegum became sentient as she kept chittering about last night. I knew it had to be, and tears rolled from my eyes as the camera panned to the charred remains of the field I'd destroyed behind her.

"The FBI's agent Thomas McMillian gave a statement earlier this morning, confirming they caught the perpetrator who died on the scene. DNA testing has identified the individual as twenty-one-year-old Jackson Reeds.

You may remember Reeds as one of the victims of the Rosary Cult, raided back in 2014. Jacksons father was the head Bishop of the cult, unfortunately taking his own life during the raid. His mother is still serving time for child abuse and child trafficking.

As for Mr. Reeds himself, he was previously seen as a successful rescue and rehabilitation story, until today."

The TV clicked off, William taking a deep breath beneath me, "That's enough of that, Dee."

"Holy shit," I whispered, my voice hoarse like I'd been screaming. I could feel myself shaking, still feel my skin burning like I was still kneeling in front of the corn.

My arms were wrapped in itchy gauze, and I wanted to tear it off. I wanted one of my salves to ease the pain, not the meds I was certain were responsible for the rubbery numbness in my system. Before I could muster up anything else, the partition swung open, making me jump.

"Hello again Ms. Bates." The same young Doc from before was offering a small smile.

"Darcy," William and I both corrected at once, and I felt his chest tense behind me with held back laughter.

"Right. Darcy," The Doc corrected, eyeing William before looking back at my chart. "This time you were out long enough to take the full bag of fluids I prescribed, which is good. That will also explain why you're shivering; I'll have the nurse bring in an extra blanket. As for your burns," he paused, a look on his face that I couldn't quite place.

He placed my chart on the counter, reaching forwards to unwrap my right arm, and even I froze in shock. The skin was pink, my hair singed off. But I was fine. William's heartbeat ticked faster against my spine, but the Doc cleared his throat, composing himself.

"Well. Let me just say, it's nothing short of a miracle. They were third degree when you came in but now..." he trailed off, not needing to explain further.

I zoned out as he rattled off other details I didn't really care about. X-rays, ointments, smoke inhalation. I just wanted to go home. Brew up something to feel better—

My chest burned as I swallowed the tiny sob threatening to break loose. But tears were already dripping down my cheeks again, making the Doc finally shut up.

"...I'll have a nurse swing by again," he said quietly, turning to leave as I swiped the tears off my face. "Please ensure you take the proper amount of time to rest. Your lungs need it."

The partition swished shut behind him, William already tucking my face against his chest. This time I was crying outright, mourning a loss he would never understand.

I'd destroyed my land, not protected it. I'd burnt it to a crisp, felt it

175

fighting and dying inside my own body. That's why I was in so much pain. I turned my magic into a weapon, and used it directly against the source which gave me such power. The give and take between us would never exist again. The land would heal, but she would never trust my bloodline again. And I would remain empty. That was the price I would pay.

William quietly took care of the nurses when they came by, even getting my discharge papers brought to us to sign so he didn't have to leave my side. He didn't even argue when I unwrapped the gauze from my sore arms, just wrapped his coat around my shoulders. It dwarfed my body as he led me out, his hand firm in mine. The only thing that restored some of my body heat was his touch, so for once, I didn't fight him.

Didn't fight him when he helped me step up into his truck. Didn't fight him as he carried me into my house, settling me on the couch and disappearing into my kitchen. Tonic trotted after him, and Gin curled up on the sofa at my feet. The poor girl was as exhausted as I was, making little snorts in her sleep.

I could tell by the scent that he was brewing lavender tea. Was he even aware that what he chose to brew was the exact remedy I would make for someone in emotional distress? Probably not.

When he brought it to me, I cupped the mug in my hands, finally arguing lightly against him and standing back up. I didn't want to be inside, I already felt so hallow.

He was a shadow at my back, his presence steady as I pushed out my screened porch and into my backyard. The sun was low, casting the first golden slants of twilight over my now dead roses. The red and pink blooms were scattered and rain beaten on the stone path, the stems draining to the same grey at the sharp thorns.

The breeze was whispering softly through the trees, many of their leaves having turned bruising over the past few days and decorating the dark ground. I picked one up, spinning it slowly by the stem, then drop it back down. It wilted to my feet, as empty of life as I felt.

"Dee?" William finally spoke to me directly, pressing closer into my space. "Do you want to tell me what's going on?" I forced a swallow, throat burning with more unshed tears.

"It's gone." I hated how my voice broke. "My magic is gone."

"...Are you sure about that?" He asked, voice so warm and genuine that it made me guilty for wanting to scream at him. Of course, I was sure. I had shattered everything, every branch of connection and trust when I became just like everyone else and destroyed a piece of my planet for a short-term gain.

"Darcy, turn around." I shook my head, tired, broken, but he wasn't having it. His hand gripped my wrist, whipping me around. This time I did curse at him, took a breath to yell—but was cut off the instant he gripped my chin, directing my gaze back the way I'd come.

Moss had bloomed in the shape of my footsteps on the stone path. The roses, still dead and out of season, had shifted to a deep evergreen where I'd touched. The ivy framing my back door was slowly unfurling, the breeze which shot across my yard when I gasped tossing it in the evening light.

"You talk about this give and take balance to your life a lot," William murmured, resting his chin on the top of my head as his arms circled my waist from behind.

"I don't think you even realize how much. But what I saw last night was a woman willing to risk giving absolutely everything. I have no idea how any of this works," he says with a light laugh. "But I doubt you would be punished by having your magic taken away."

I lifted a palm, feeling the autumn breeze curve over it, and snake its way into my sleeve in a caress.

Are we...?

The wind rose, warm despite the chill to the air, twirling through my trees until the sky was painted red and gold. I reached a hand up, William's meeting mine as we caught the same leaf, fingers brushing.

Gin and Tonic were seated in the kitchen window, grooming and sunning themselves. They occasionally glanced in our direction, taking in the world as it continued to ebb and flow around us.

Leaves skirted across the ground in tandem, dancing and twisting away on the whispering wind. The creak of the old dogwood groaned a low baritone against the call of a distant crow. And the sky slowly bleached to grey as the sun continued its descent behind the mountain ridge.

We stood there until the stars winked down from the growing darkness, the moon bright in her ascent. I loved the world like this. Quiet. Thick. Caving in on itself until only its seams were left. The weaving threads of give and take at its center, which made everything alive possible.

Acknowledgements

This project was nothing short of a whirlwind, and it would not have been possible without the wonderful community of bookish creators around me. Thank you to the ARC readers who made the time to view this within a week so I could still release it for Halloween. Special thanks to the wonderful Atlas Creed for helping me navigate a new genre and audience. And a giant shoutout and thank you to MG Designs for managing to find the time to create a custom chapter header of Gin and Tonic!

And as always, thank you to my wonderful husband for enduring the absolute chaos this project was—and for debuting as a cover model! I love you so much.

To my readers: thank you for continuing to support me on my writing journey. I love the freedom of genre hopping, and I hope to continue to deliver entertaining stories for you no matter what shelves you find me on. Without you, none of this magic would be possible.

Nightshade

www.ingramcontent.com/pod-product-compliance
Lightning Source LLC
Chambersburg PA
CBHW050334110726
47899CB00007B/2500